PRAIRIE WOLVES

When Bender County, Kansas, becomes the target of a callous gang of range thieves, deputy sheriff Brad Harper finds himself at the forefront of the action. Upon learning that his friend is missing, Harper rides out to his ranch to look for clues and finds the place ablaze. Harper's troubles do not end here, though, and much blood will be shed before justice is done.

CORBA SUNMAN

PRAIRIE WOLVES

Complete and Unabridged

LINFORD
Leicester

First published in Great Britain in 2010 by
Robert Hale Limited
London

First Linford Edition
published 2011
by arrangement with
Robert Hale Limited
London

British Library CIP Data

Sunman, Corba.
   Prairie wolves. - - (Linford western library)
   1. Western stories.
   2. Large type books.
   I. Title II. Series
   823.9′2–dc22

   ISBN 978–1–4448–0792–9

Published by
F. A. Thorpe (Publishing)
Anstey, Leicestershire

Set by Words & Graphics Ltd.
Anstey, Leicestershire
Printed and bound in Great Britain by
T. J. International Ltd., Padstow, Cornwall

This book is printed on acid-free paper

1

As the shadows of night closed in, Deputy Sheriff Brad Harper rode his buckskin out of Sweet Spring, Kansas, and headed west across the undulating range. The darkness did not bother him as he made for the Bar Franch, where his friend, Bob Fuller ran a small herd of cattle. Bob's sister, Lily-Beth, had ridden into town that afternoon with the disturbing news that Bob had spotted two strangers on his grass the day before, had ridden out to check on them, and had not returned. Lily-Beth was concerned that some mishap had befallen her brother.

Harper, a tall, tough man in his middle twenties, brown-eyed, broad-shouldered and powerfully built, was one of two deputies who enforced county law under the direction of Sheriff Mort Bland. The trouble that had hit Bender County was similar to the mayhem which had occurred to the east a year back, around the building of the railroad, but as no railroad line was planned through Bender County — not even a spur — the reason for the outbreak of lawlessness was a mystery.

Sheriff Bland had been out with a posse when Lily-Beth arrived in town, and Harper tried to get the girl to wait until he could accompany her back to the Bar F, but she was strong-minded as well as beautiful, with her long blonde hair and blue eyes, and wanted to be at home should her brother return. Harper hoped to marry Lily-Beth in the near future and, in view of the trouble on the range, was worried because she had ridden out alone. The sheriff had returned from a fruitless search for strangers reported to be lurking out of town, and Harper had taken out immediately to chase after his sweetheart.

The Bar F ranch was fifteen miles west of Clear Spring and Harper rode as fast as he dared in the night but failed to see Lily-Beth on the trail. The moon showed from behind a distant bluff, and his range of vision had increased imperceptibly by the time he reached the cluster of ranch buildings that was the headquarters of the little cattle ranch. The shadowy landscape brooding under the silver light of the moon seemed unreal. Shadows were as black as ink, and the night breeze, coming all the way from the distant Rockies, blew strongly into Harper's angular face.

He reined in quickly when he spotted flaring light arising from the buildings ahead, and saw wisps of smoke billowing up to smear the clean night air in an eerie scene that was a rancher's worst nightmare — a ranch fire!

Harper sank his spurs into the buckskin's flanks and sent the big horse galloping towards the ranch, hoofs thudding on the hard range. As he turned into the yard a gunflash split the shadows from near the house and a bullet crackled over his head. Two more guns opened up almost immediately from either side of the house, and Harper dived out of his saddle and rolled on the hardpan. He drew his pistol and narrowed his eyes to pierce the gloom. Dancing flames showed at the ground floor windows of the house, and he caught a glimpse of movement on the porch as a figure became silhouetted against the growing conflagration.

He refrained from shooting because he had no idea who was in the yard. Then he heard a thin scream and recognized Lily-Beth's voice. He got to his feet and ran forward, gun ready, his big figure hunched over to lessen his target area, and caught a fleeting glimpse of a slender figure struggling in the grip of a larger, man-sized figure.

Hoofs pounded somewhere in the background and receded quickly. Lily-Beth was struggling with the man in front of the house. Harper ran forward, his gun upraised. He saw Lily-Beth suddenly fall to the ground, and fired swiftly as the man turned to flee. The gunflash ripped through the shadows and the shot hammered out a string of echoes across the dark range. The man fell to the ground and remained motionless. Harper ran to Lily-Beth's side, holstering his gun as he dropped to his knees beside her.

'Lily-Beth, are you OK?' he demanded.

The girl stirred and lifted a hand to her forehead. She was breathing heavily.

'Brad, is that you?' she demanded tremulously. 'Thank God you are here! I should have taken your advice and waited in town for you.'

'What happened?' He straightened and helped her up. 'It looks like we can't save the house,' he observed, and led her back from the searing heat.

An explosion sounded somewhere in the house and a great flaring gout of flame shot skywards. The fire seemed to roar up in a frightening crescendo, and burning debris began to fall around them.

'That was your supply of kerosene going up,' Harper said. 'Have you seen anything of Bob?'

'No. He wasn't home when I got back. Then three men came. They had gunny sacks on their heads with eyeholes cut in them. They frightened me — shouting and threatening. One of them held me outside while the other two set fire to the house. I tried to get away because the man holding me said they were going to kill me. What is happening, Brad? Why are we getting this trouble? It has always been so peaceful around here.'

'I've no idea what's going on,' Harper replied grimly, 'but I sure as hell intend to find out. Stay close to me, Lily. I want to check on that guy I shot.'

'I won't let you out of my sight after this,' Lily-Beth said fervently.

Harper turned to the huddled figure lying on the hard ground. The light from the burning house illuminated the dead man's features and Harper dropped to one knee to look intently in an attempt at recognition, but the man was a stranger.

'Is he dead?' Lily-Beth's voice trembled with fear. She pressed close to Harper, her face looking unreal in the uncertain light from the fire. There was fear in her tone and her expression was a mask of apprehension. She was frightened, but made an effort to regain her composure.

'I never missed a shot in my life,' Harper responded harshly.

'I got a good look at all three when they showed up, despite their masks, and hadn't seen any of them before,' she declared. 'What do you think has happened to Bob? I didn't want him to ride out when he saw those strangers, but you know Bob — you can't change his mind when it's made up.'

'I'll go out and look for him when the sun comes up,' Harper said. 'He'll have left tracks. I'll get to the bottom of this, don't you worry.'

He turned his head to the right and peered off into the shadows.

'What is it?' Lily-Beth demanded in a scared tone.

'I can hear horses coming. Three of them, I guess. Jump on my buckskin, Lil, and ride out of here while I confront them. It might be more of the men who fired the place. Go out to that stand of cottonwoods by the stream and wait there until I come for you.'

'Be careful, Brad,' she whispered.

'Sure,' he responded. 'Get out of here quick and be quiet about it.'

Lily-Beth turned and ran to where the buckskin was standing with trailing reins. She swung into the saddle and rode out of the yard. Harper watched her departure until she was lost in the shadows. The sound of the approaching riders had grown louder, and he ran to his right to avoid being silhouetted by the burning house. He dropped into cover, facing the direction of the newcomers, and presently saw three riders materializing out of the gloom.

'Hold it right there,' Harper called. 'Who are you?'

The trio reined in and sat motionless in their saddles. Harper could see the figures but they were too far out to be identified in the flickering light of the fire.

'That sounds like Brad Harper,' one of the men declared, and Harper lowered his gun when he recognized the voice.

'Abe Hickman,' he responded. 'What in hell are you doing here at this time? Did you see the men who rode out?'

'We were out riding the range because strangers have been seen,' Hickman replied, 'and I spotted the fire from the rise by Water Gully. We also heard shooting, Brad, so what the hell is going on? Who fired the house?'

The trio of riders came forward, and Harper gazed at the blocky figure of Abe Hickman, who owned the big AH ranch immediately to the north of Bar F. Hickman stepped down from his horse and faced Harper, whose back was to the fire. Hickman stood less than six feet, and was dwarfed by Harper's height and bulk, but he was a tough man, seemingly made of leather and

9

coffin nails. He listened intently to Harper's explanation of events.

'So it looks like they got Fuller,' Hickman observed. 'It was a damn-fool thing to do; riding out alone after those strangers. I heard about the range-stealing last year back east around the railroad, and it looks like the same thing is starting up here. But I ain't gonna stand still and let anyone rob me blind. No one is gonna move in on this range without a hell of a fight. My outfit will be on guard after this, and God help anyone trying to muscle in.' He paused, and then added as an afterthought: 'Where is Lily-Beth? Is she OK?'

'She's all right. I sent her out when I heard you coming. I'll take her into town, leave her there, and get back here by sunup. I plan to look for Bob's tracks and trail him to where he's at.'

'You'll probably find him dead on the range if those strangers he was after are a part of the gang that operated east of here,' Hickman mused. 'I'll ride into town tomorrow and have a word with the sheriff.' He turned back to his horse. 'There's nothing we can do here, it looks like. If you want, you can have a couple of my boys to ride with you tomorrow.'

'Thanks, but I can handle it,' Harper replied. 'Thanks for the offer. If we get big trouble then we'll surely need help later on.'

'We'll be ready.' Hickman swung into his saddle, turned his horse and rode out.

'So long,' Harper called, and watched the trio fade into the night.

He stood motionless, gazing around into the shadows, his ears filled with the crackling of the fire as sun-dried woodwork burned furiously. Smoke was billowing up into the night sky and the attendant flames chased through the gloom, making the darkness uncertain. The motionless figure of the man he had shot attracted his gaze and he crossed to it, dropped to one knee, and looked again at the immobile features. He shook his head, wondering at the motive for the fire because the man was a stranger, but there had to be a reason why he had risked his life to cause trouble.

Realizing that there was no point in musing over unknown facts, Harper looked around. He spotted a horse standing by the rail surrounding the yard and fetched it so that he could load the dead man across the saddle. Leading the horse, he went to the corral to saddle a mount for Lily-Beth, walked the animals out of the yard, and headed for the cottonwoods near the stream. He needed to alert the sheriff to what was going on, and in the morning he would track down Bob Fuller, or discover what had happened to his friend.

When he reached the trees he called softly to Lily-Beth. When there was no reply, and no sign of the girl or his buckskin, he frowned and called louder, to be mocked by the sighing of the night breeze blowing through the trees.

'Lily-Beth!' he called sharply. 'This ain't the time to be playing tricks.

Come on out. We're going back to town, but fast. I need to alert the sheriff to what's happened here.'

Silence followed his words and he looked into the shadows, his mind jangling with alarm as he finally accepted that the girl was not around. He looked towards the burning ranch, now just a ragged pool of red brilliance in the anonymous background of the night, and felt a sense of uneasiness as he considered. Lily-Beth would never have ridden away voluntarily. So those two men who fled from the ranch upon his arrival must have awaited their opportunity to grab her when she rode out, and now she and they could be anywhere.

He was reluctant to face the grim fact, hoping against hope that Lily-Beth might suddenly call to announce her presence, but he was aware that he had to move the situation along. He swung into the saddle of Lily-Beth's mount, tied the reins of the lead horse carrying the dead man to the saddle horn, and headed out for Clear Spring, filled with misgiving because he was riding away from the girl he loved.

Harper had not travelled far when he gained the uneasy feeling that he was not alone on the range. He continued riding, but loosened the big pistol in his holster and peered around into the shadows. He heard nothing suspicious. The night was silent and still except for the hoofbeats of the horses with him and the creak of saddle leather. He reined in suddenly and sat with strained ears, listening for sounds. When he caught the thud and beat of hoofs on his back trail, which cut off suddenly, almost in midstride, he knew his instincts had not betrayed him.

He was being stalked! He drew his gun as he slid from the saddle and stood between the two horses, listening intently. The night breeze whistled around the brim of his Stetson and he pushed it back off his forehead. There was no noise in the surrounding darkness. He cocked his gun, certain he was about to be assailed, and moved a few strides away from the horses, fully alert now and ready for trouble.

Tense minutes passed. He dropped to one knee and waited, motionless and silent, deadly as a rattlesnake disturbed in its nest. The two horses were cropping now, tearing at the lush grass with their teeth, and he moved further to his right, keeping low, eager for any action which might lead him to Lily-Beth. His eyes began to water in the breeze but he remained motionless, staring into the shadows, his emotions rolled into a ball and pushed into the back of his mind.

When he heard a soft footfall in the grass he heaved a silent sigh. Come and get me, he thought, and flattened himself slowly, hugging the ground and facing the direction from which sounds were emanating. His eyes were accustomed to the night but his range of vision was less than five yards. He waited, breathing shallowly through his open mouth, and when he caught an indistinct movement, just a faint changing of shadow patterns, he clenched his teeth, aware that he desperately needed a prisoner; someone who might be able to enlighten him as to what was going on.

A man materialized from the gloom, faint moonlight glinting on a pistol he was holding. He was making for the horses cropping the grass, and was not facing Harper directly but angling a few feet to Harper's right. He almost stepped on Harper's left hand as he passed by so close that Harper thought his own breathing might be overheard. But the man was intent on the horses, his whole attention fixed on getting close without being discovered.

Harper waited until the figure had gone on a couple of yards, then gained his feet soundlessly. He lunged forward and struck with the long barrel of his pistol, slamming the solid metal against the man's right ear with a sickening thud. The man collapsed with a gasping groan. Harper stepped in close and bent to snatch up a discarded pistol. He heaved a long sigh as he searched the man for other weapons, removed a long-bladed knife from a sheath, and then moved out of arm's length to await the man's return to consciousness.

Minutes passed before the man uttered a long-drawn groan and began to stir. When he sat up, Harper revealed his presence with a low warning for the man to remain still. The man froze, a hand to his head, and then looked around to see Harper's ominous figure and a levelled pistol pointing at him.

'You were stalking me,' Harper said. 'So tell me about it.'

'Who are you?' the man demanded. 'You had no cause to hit me.'

'You were sneaking up on me with a gun in your hand; your intention was plain. I guess you are one of the men who fired the Bar F ranch earlier, so what happened to the girl at the spread?'

'I don't know anything about that,' the man replied.

'What's your name?' Harper countered.

'Jim Boldra. I'm riding from Wichita to Dodge City.'

'Where's your horse?'

'Back there.'

'So why were you stalking me?' Harper persisted.

'Is that a law star you're wearing?'

'It is. I'm Brad Harper, a deputy sheriff out of Clear Spring. You've made a bad mistake trying for me. I'll take you into town and jail you until you can come up with a reason why you were out here afoot with your gun out and heading for my horses, no doubt hoping to get the drop on me. So let us take it from there. What was going on?'

'I got nothing to say. I don't know what you're talking about. I ain't seen any trouble hereabouts.'

'We'll go and pick up your horse. You'll have time to reflect on your situation during the ride to Clear Spring. Get up and start moving, and don't try anything if you want to remain in one piece.'

Boldra got slowly to his feet, holding a hand to his head. He staggered as he set off back the way he had come and Harper followed him closely, his pistol levelled. They covered fifty yards before a horse whinnied in the shadows ahead.

'Are you riding alone?' Harper demanded.

'Yeah, I'm job-hunting.'

'Get your horse and we'll head for town.'

They walked on to the horse and Harper led it back to where his horses were waiting. Boldra, ahead with his hands raised, halted abruptly when he saw the dead man draped across a saddle. Harper jabbed him with the muzzle of his pistol.

'Keep moving. You're lucky I got the drop on you or you'd be dead now, face down across your saddle.'

'Who is he?' Boldra asked.

'I don't know. He was with two other men. They fired the Bar F ranch house, and this one had hold of a girl. He told her they would kill her.'

'And you stopped them?' Boldra asked.

'That's right. Now quit asking questions. Get down on the grass on your face and put your hands above your head. Don't make any sudden movements because I'm feeling a mite hair-triggered at the moment.'

Boldra got down on his belly and placed his hands above his head, palms down. Harper kept one eye on him as he moved around the two horses, and by so doing missed a sudden movement on the far side of the animal carrying the dead man. The shadows exploded into flame and noise as a pistol blasted, and Harper felt the fiery bite of hot lead tearing through the flesh of his left arm just below the shoulder. He whirled away instinctively, dropping to the ground, and thrust up his pistol. But the flash of the shot had dazzled him and he could see nothing beyond an orange glare.

The pistol fired again but Harper was

moving fast, rolling away from danger, his face averted. He heard the crackle of a slug passing by his left ear and blinked rapidly to improve his sight. His prisoner was shouting in the background, and he guessed these were the two men who had fired the Bar F. He cursed himself for not checking out the situation more carefully.

Boldra collided with Harper in a diving lunge, his outstretched arms encircling Harper's body around the waist. Harper half-turned like a cat, and slammed his pistol into Boldra's face. Boldra groaned and spun away, cursing. The man beside the two horses fired his pistol again, and Boldra yelled at him, telling him to hold his fire.

Harper flicked up his pistol and returned the shot, aiming for the muzzle flame of the Colt. He heard a thin cry of agony which cut through the blasting report, and eased away to find Boldra and cover him. Boldra was staggering around, his hands to his face. Harper surged to within arm's

21

length and swung his left fist in a powerful hook. His raw-boned knuckles slammed against Boldra's jaw with a satisfactory meat-chopping sound. Boldra went down as if he had been pole-axed, and Harper straightened, his pistol levelled at the hip.

Pain was jabbing through his left arm and he could feel blood running from his wound, but he ignored the discomfort and went to his horses. He could see the inert figure of a man lying on the grass near the uneasy animals, saw the glint of moonlight on metal, and picked up a discarded pistol. He backed off and looked around, ready for more trouble, but the surrounding night was silent and his sixth sense subsided.

His thoughts roved over the sequence of events, and he was surprised by the speed with which trouble had taken hold. Bob Fuller had disappeared, and in the space of a few short hours all hell had broken loose. Now here he was standing alone on the deserted range with a dead man and two prisoners, the

Bar F ranch house had burned down, and Lily-Beth was missing. He was greatly bothered by the girl's disappearance, and his frustration was aggravated by the grim fact that there was nothing he could do to restore the situation until the sun came up.

He prepared to go on. He checked the unknown man lying beside the horses and found him still alive but apparently hard hit, with a dark splotch of blood showing on his right side just below the ribcage. Blood was leaking steadily from the bullet hole. Harper shook his head, aware that he could not take the man on to town in such a serious condition. He would have to be left and picked up by a wagon. He bent over Boldra, found the man returning to his senses, and shook him roughly to hasten his recovery. Boldra groaned and slumped back when Harper pulled him to his feet, but Harper persisted, sensing that the man was foxing in an attempt to gain an advantage.

'Do you still deny being involved in

this trouble?' Harper demanded when Boldra eventually sat up in full control of his senses.

'I ain't mixed up in anything,' Boldra replied obstinately. 'I jumped you because there was a chance of getting away.'

'And a lot of good it did you.' Harper grinned. 'You're still on your way to jail so get on your horse and we'll head on in to Clear Spring. Come the morning, you'll be sleeping your head off behind bars, but I've got to be back out here again before the sun shows, so don't give me any more trouble because the next time you try anything I'll gut-shoot you.'

He removed his neckerchief, tied it tightly around the wound in his upper arm and then prepared to ride on. His thoughts were bleak. He was fired up and ready for anything, but tension gripped him and it was aggravated by a feeling of helplessness because he had ridden away from the spot where Lily-Beth vanished. He dared not dwell upon the girl's whereabouts or what might have happened to her, but was consoled by the knowledge that when daylight came he would enter Hell itself to find her.

2

Clear Spring was dark and silent when Harper eventually reached the main street. There was a light showing in the front window of the law office and he rode towards it, echoes rising up from the hoofs of the horses. The time must be after midnight, he assumed, and he slid wearily from his saddle in front of the jail. He pulled his gun as Boldra dismounted, and urged his prisoner into the office. Sheriff Mort Bland was dozing at his desk; he started up when Harper called him and reached for his holstered gun.

Mort Bland was well into his fifties. His hair was iron grey and his lined face showed the dire effects of law dealing over twenty years. He was tall and thin. His blue eyes were deep-set and filled with a brightness which indicated that nothing surprised him these days, for he had seen everything that could possibly happen since first pinning on a law badge. He got to his feet and came around the desk, his keen gaze assessing the prisoner. Harper explained what had occurred out at Bar F, and Bland listened without interruption, his gaze never leaving Boldra's expressionless face.

'I'm heading right back to Bar F,' Harper finished. 'I've got to get on Lily-Beth's trail as soon as the sun comes up.'

'You'd better take a couple of posse men with you,' Bland suggested. 'And let Doc Carter take a look at your arm before you ride out.' He turned to his desk and picked up a bunch of keys. 'Let's put your prisoner behind bars and then we'll talk. I've gone through the reports of that bad trouble east of here a year ago, and after what's gone on in the county today I'm inclined to believe it is the same gang, working this way.'

'I thought about that immediately

Lily-Beth said Bob had gone missing,' Harper mused, 'but the trouble last year was connected with the railroad, and we are not scheduled for rail tracks coming in this direction.'

'There were two surveyors through here last year,' Bland recalled.

'Yeah, but they said they had an easier route north of here to Dodge City. They didn't reckon on pushing rails through Bender County.'

Boldra was locked in a cell. Harper led the way back into the front office, and paused when he saw the street door opening. His eyes narrowed to mere slits when he recognized the tall, broad figure of Joss Kemp, Bender County's second deputy, coming into the office. Kemp was big in every way, his powerful figure muscular. He had big hands and feet, and his head seemed too large for his body; also his nose and mouth were bigger than normal. The only thing small about him was his eyes — piglike and filled with an innate cunning. He was dressed in a brown store suit and wore a cartridge belt with holstered pistol on his right.

'What have you been up to?' Kemp demanded, slamming the street door and pausing on the threshold to look aggressively at Harper. 'There's a dead man across a saddle out front. Where did you pick him up? How come you can ride out of town and find some action while I'm always stuck in the background, eating your dust and picking up the pieces? So what's going on that I should know about?'

'There's nothing you need to concern yourself about, Joss.' Sheriff Bland came into the office and dumped the cell keys on a corner of the desk. He dropped wearily into his seat. 'Leave the dirty work to Brad and me. What have you found out about those men who rode into town this evening? What's their line of business?'

'I was talking to a couple of them in the saloon,' Kemp said. 'They're a pretty close-mouthed bunch. But it seems they are on the level. They are setting up a sawmill on the edge of town, seeing we ain't got one. They plan to supply wooden buildings of all kinds, everything from a shack to a church. It's gonna be a big operation. Their boss man, Norton Calder, will be turning up here in a few days. He's gonna handle the sales and oversee the work. They are renting those old sheds by the creek. I heard them doing a deal with Ben Tarrant. He owns those sheds, and said he'd be pleased to get some rent from them.'

'Close-mouthed, you said!' Bland smiled. 'It sounds like they talked their heads off. Well, stick around them and learn all you can. We've got too many strangers in the county at this time so keep a close eye on them. I want to know exactly what their plans are and whether they are on the level.'

'So what's the trouble on the range?' Kemp persisted. 'Did you find Bob Fuller, Brad?'

'No.' Harper shook his head. 'I'll get my arm checked by the doctor and then head back to Bar F, Mort. I need to be ready to track down Lily as soon as the sun shows.'

'Will someone tell me what is going on?' Kemp rasped.

'Mort will tell you,' Harper replied. 'I'm pushed for time.'

'Watch your step out there,' Bland warned.

'Sure.' Harper forced a grin and departed. He walked along the street to the doctor's house and rapped sharply on the front door. He was about to repeat the summons when a bedroom window creaked open and Doc Carter demanded his business.

'It's Brad Harper, Doc. Sorry to bother you at this time but I stopped a slug in my arm earlier, and I have to be riding out again soon as I can. Will you tend to me before I leave?'

'Sure, Brad. Give me a minute, huh?'

Harper leaned against a doorpost and looked around the darkened street, stifling a yawn. His mind was simmering with concern for Lily-Beth, and dawn could not arrive soon enough for him. He saw lamplight flare in the window of the doctor's ground-floor office, then the front door was unbolted and Doc Carter came out to the doorstep.

'Come in, Brad. Are you bad hurt?'

'It hurts like hell, Doc, but I don't think it is serious. I wouldn't have bothered you until tomorrow, but I've got some more night riding to do and I may not get back here for a couple of days — long enough for a wound to turn bad, huh?'

'You can't be too careful with gunshot wounds,' Carter observed. 'Did you find Bob Fuller?'

'I didn't get a chance to look for him.' Harper explained the incidents which had occurred out at Bar F, and saw the doctor shake his head when he mentioned Lily-Beth's disappearance.

'I don't like the sound of that,' Carter mused. 'So you're going back out there to start looking for tracks at first light, huh? I guess you heard all about the trouble they had further east. Do you reckon it is the same gang at work here?'

'I'll keep an open mind until I've done some checking up. You better know that I left a badly wounded man out on the range on the trail about three miles this side of Bar F. He would have died if I'd loaded him on a horse so I made him comfortable and reckoned to send a wagon out for him.' Harper sat down by a small table and rolled up his left sleeve. Blood had congealed around a deep bullet slash in the flesh on the outer edge of the arm.

'I'll ride out and check that man when you leave, Brad,' Carter observed. 'Will you wait for me?'

'Sure, but I think you'll have the ride for nothing. I expect that galoot will be dead before morning.'

'I couldn't live with myself if I didn't take the trouble to check him out.' Carter busied himself, and Harper sat motionless, thinking of Lily-Beth while the doctor cleansed and then bandaged his wound. 'There you are,' Carter said when he'd finished. 'It'll soon be as good as new. I'll get my medical bag and fetch my grey from the livery barn. See you at the barn in ten minutes, huh? I hope you'll find Bob and Lily-Beth in good health, Brad.'

'I'll find them, Doc!' Harper got to his feet and rolled down his sleeve. 'I've got to get moving fast. Thanks. I'll see you in ten minutes at the barn. I'm gonna ride fast so come prepared, huh?'

He departed and headed back to the law office. Kemp was leading the horse bearing the corpse away along the street, and Harper shook his head as he studied the big deputy's receding figure. He had never liked Kemp, having found the man lacking in some of the qualities essential to good law enforcement. Kemp was a natural bully. He was inclined to shoot first, even in situations which did not merit the use of a gun, and Harper even suspected Kemp of being responsible for some of the petty crimes which had occurred around the county in recent months. Several eyewitness reports gave a description of a suspect which tallied closely with Kemp's general build.

Mort Bland was standing in the doorway of the law office, shaking his head.

'Joss reckons I should send him out to Bar F instead of you, Brad,' Bland said. 'He thinks you are too personally involved with Bob and Lily-Beth to keep a good perspective on developments.'

'No chance!' Harper exclaimed. 'I wouldn't trust him to do anything I couldn't oversee.'

'You've never liked him,' Bland grimaced, 'and I can't say I'd want him doing anything but minor duties.'

'You'd be doing right by firing him,' Harper said. 'I'd better be riding, Mort.'

'Sure. Do what you have to. I hope you'll find Lily-Beth in good health when you locate her. I'm thinking of sending out a posse later to back you up so leave a good trail for them to follow, huh?'

'I'll do that. Doc is riding with me to check on that wounded man out on the range, and if the guy is still alive then Doc can get a wagon from Bar F and bring him to town.'

'It looks like you've thought of everything. Good hunting, Brad.'

Harper nodded and turned to his horse. He tightened the cinch and stepped up into the saddle. For a moment he sat looking around the darkened street, his thoughts unpleasant as he considered what he had to do. He was badly shocked by what had occurred out at Bar F, but his judgement was unclouded, and he touched spurs to the flanks of the horse and set the animal into a canter. As he passed the livery barn Doc Carter rode out to join him, and they left town together.

There was little conversation between them as they crossed the darkened range. Doc Carter was accustomed to riding alone and in silence around the county and Harper had his fears for Lily-Beth to contend with. The night sky changed almost imperceptibly as time passed, and when they were within a few miles of the Bar F Harper began to look around for landmarks. He had a good idea where he had left the wounded man, and eventually he led the doctor almost directly to the spot.

Harper remained in his saddle while the doctor examined the motionless figure lying in gras. Carter did not need more than a cursory glance before straightening.

'He's dead,' Carter said.

'I guessed he would be.' Harper shifted impatiently in his saddle. He could see the sky turning grey to the east and knew sunup was barely an hour away. 'I need to push on, Doc. I'm sorry you've had this long ride for nothing.'

'It's all part of the job,' Carter replied. 'I'll head off to John Bessey's place. I need to look in on his wife, and

37

I'll get a good breakfast there. Take care, Brad, and good luck.'

Harper went on, and approached the Bar F cautiously when he reached there. Dawn was close at hand, the shadows of the night receding. He eased his pistol in its holster and held his reins in his left hand when he reached the gate. There was the smell of burning in the air, and he could see wisps of smoke still rising from the charred heap that had been the ranch house.

He was tired and hungry, but he ignored his discomfort and waited for enough daylight in which to begin his duty.

As soon as he could see to check tracks, Harper rode out to the cotton-woods by the stream and cast around for the prints of his buckskin. When he did not find them he backtracked towards the ranch, using the line he figured Lily-Beth would have taken the night before. He had barely covered fifty yards when he spotted hoofprints which he immediately recognized as having been made by the buckskin; he compressed his lips when he saw another set of prints at the same spot. Someone had waited just outside the ranch yard and confronted Lily-Beth when she rode out.

Harper saw that the two sets of tracks went on together, and he wished he had been aware of the fact hours before. An expert tracker, he travelled at a canter, studying the prints as he rode. When he found them heading northwest he considered the country in that direction and knew that Abe Hickman's AH ranch stretched for miles beyond the Bar F boundary. He continued, filled with impatience because he needed to get to Lily-Beth, and yet the grim chore of finding the missing Bob Fuller should have had priority.

He came across another set of tracks which joined the two sets of prints he was following. He reined in to study them and attempt to work out the significance of their presence. The three sets of tracks went on together, and

Harper wondered just how many riders had taken part in the attack on Bar F. He pushed on fast, filled with foreboding.

When the trail skirted a trading post set on a level stretch of a well-used trail which led eventually to Dodge City, miles to the north-east, Harper saw that one of the sets of prints turned aside and headed around to the back of the store. He reined to the left, dismounted at a rail in front of the low building, and went to enter the gloomy store. He paused on the threshold to enable his eyes to become accustomed to the shadowy interior. He caught a movement beyond the bar and saw Dack Hoose, the trader, sorting through a pile of merchandise.

Harper had confronted Hoose on several occasions in the past in the course of his investigations into local crime, and suspected the man of making a business of receiving stolen goods, knowing them to have been stolen, although he had never found any proof of Hoose's guilt. A solitary, sullen man, Hoose seemed to make a living from his business although the trading post always appeared to be deserted — there were not many cattle spreads in the area to really warrant a business out here in the back of beyond, and Hoose always charged more for his goods than did the general store in Clear Spring.

'Huh, what are you doing out this way?' Hoose demanded, his voice sounding like gravel being washed in a pan. He was short and fleshy, with a bulging waistline. His almost square face had protruding ears and a snub nose, and his lank, greying hair looked as if it had not been washed or combed in a month. 'Has something gone missing around Clear Spring? I reckon I'm the first man you think of checking out. Say, I'm getting a mite tired of being the prime suspect on your list, Harper.'

'You've told me you always sleep light,' Harper replied. 'So did you hear three riders passing through here during the night?'

'I can't say that I did! And if I had I wouldn't stick my nose into their business if they was riding through. Who are you chasing now?'

'Did anyone stop off here during the night?' Harper persisted.

'No, and I ain't seen any strangers around for at least a week. Don't tell me the bank in Clear Spring has been robbed again! You ain't caught the thieves who robbed it the last time. Haw! Haw! Haw!'

'Change your tune mighty quick, Hoose, or you'll be nursing a fat lip and missing some teeth when I ride on,' Harper said stiffly.

Hoose let his face slip into an aggressive expression. 'Don't come around here throwing your weight about,' he declared. 'I'm on my own property here, and I don't take anything from anyone. You come in here to ride me and I'll make you wish you hadn't left town.'

'That would be the biggest mistake

you'd ever make.' Harper smiled. 'So what have you got to hide? Why are you lying about nobody stopping off here? I'm trailing three riders who passed by in the night, and one of them turned in at the back of this place. I checked the tracks before I came in. So tell me about it.'

'That doesn't mean a thing.' Hoose shrugged his heavy shoulders. 'Anybody wanting anything during the night, when I'm asleep, can stop off in my barn and pick up general supplies. I leave stuff out there that a passer-by might need, and they leave their dough. That way they don't have to disturb me or wait around till sunup. I trust folk to play fair with my arrangement, and usually they don't let me down.'

Harper shook his head in disbelief. 'I'll take a look at the tracks out back, just for the record,' he said.

'Are you calling me a liar?' Hoose demanded, scowling.

'Take it how you like! The man who stopped off here in the night was riding in the company of two other riders that I'm anxious to talk to. I need to know which way your visitor rode when he left. Do you want to make something of that?'

Hoose gazed at Harper for some moments, his expression grim. Then he shrugged and shook his head.

'I guess you got your duty to do as you see it,' he observed grudgingly. 'Just don't make a mess in my barn.'

Harper departed by the front door and walked around the low building to the yard at the rear. He looked for hoofprints and found some which were fairly fresh. They led into the large barn beyond the yard and did not emerge again. He dropped his right hand to the butt of his holstered gun as he walked to the door of the barn which was closed. The silence pressing in around him seemed to prickle with hostility and he sensed that all was not right as he continued, his nerves stretched to breaking-point by the tension crowding into his mind.

A horse in the barn whinnied loudly as he passed a dusty front window beside the door, and in the same instant the sound of shattering glass alerted him to trouble. He drew his pistol as he hurled himself flat, rolled, and came to rest on his left side, his gun hand lifting to cover the window. He saw a bearded face framed in the glass-shattered aperture and the sun glinted on a pistol being thrust forward in his general direction. The weapon flamed and the crash of the shot hammered through the heavy silence. Harper rolled to his left, towards the wall of the barn, and pain stabbed through the bullet wound he had suffered in his left arm. But he had other things to think about at that moment and clenched his teeth when he heard a slug strike a stone and whine away over the trading post.

He thrust his gun forward and fired instinctively, aiming for the woodwork just below the window aperture. Gun-smoke flared and he fired twice more in quick succession, bracketing the small

45

area behind which he guessed the man in the barn was standing. There was no more shooting from his assailant, and he crawled to the barn door.

Gun echoes faded slowly and an uneasy silence returned. Harper thrust himself to his feet. He grasped the door and tried to pull it open but it was barred on the inside. A gun blasted inside the barn in response and a bullet splintered through the door only an inch or so away from Harper's right shoulder. He lunged to his left to clear the door and two more shots came boring through the sun-warped boards. He dived around the front left corner of the barn and dropped flat as three slugs came smashing through the boards, seeking his flesh.

Harper rolled on to his back. He took time to reload his pistol, meanwhile looking for another way into the barn. The building was well built, the boards thick, and it presented a problem for someone needing to get inside quickly without using the door. He crawled along the side of the barn to the rear corner, sweating now, and stood up when he saw a doorway in the loft; it was open. The aperture was too high for him to reach, but some packing-cases were piled haphazardly nearby and he stacked them so that he could ascend to the loft.

The cases threatened to collapse when he put his weight on them but he managed to get his fingers into the door aperture. When he tried to haul himself up into the loft his left arm hurt so badly he almost lost his grip. He clenched his teeth, ignored the pain, and forced himself up into the doorway. Sweat ran down his face, stinging his eyes, and he lay in the entrance to the loft to recover from his exertions.

A horse stamped somewhere below in the barn but there were no other sounds, and Harper eased to his feet. He could see the top of a ladder leaning against the floor of the loft where it ended overlooking the main body of the barn, but when he took a step towards the ladder the floor creaked and a gun below blasted three times, hurling spaced shots into the loft. He was not hit, but the slugs came close enough to make him halt. He listened to the dying echoes of the shooting. Gunsmoke was drifting upwards from the barn; he dropped flat and inched forward to take a look below.

He had to expose his head to observe the barn. His ears were ringing from the crash of the shooting. He cuffed sweat from his face with his left sleeve as he eased his gun forward to cover the barn, and remained motionless while he checked out the lower area. A brown horse was in a stall towards the rear, but there was no sign of the man who was shooting at him. He remained motionless, awaiting action from below.

The top of the ladder to his left began to move. Before he could react it crashed down into the barn. Harper thrust his arm into space, fired three shots into the area below, and two shots came back at him in quick response. He saw gunsmoke spurting and put two slugs into the spot. The next instant a man stepped forward stiffly from the shadows, took two staggering paces, then fell on his face. Harper remained motionless, gazing down at the man until the last of the echoes of the shooting had faded.

The man did not move again. He was lying on his face, his pistol was close to his right hand. Harper heaved a long sigh and holstered his own pistol. He gripped the edge of the floor of the loft and swung his body over to hang for a moment at arm's length before releasing his hold and dropping to the floor of the barn. Gunsmoke stung his eyes and twitched at his nostrils as he crossed to where the man was stretched out, a trickle of blood seeping from his body.

Harper kicked the pistol clear before turning the man over on to his back. He looked down into a bearded face which he did not know. The man was dead. Harper studied him for several moments, wondering who he was and why he had attacked a lawman for no apparent reason. He shook his head, puzzled by the development, and went to the door of the barn, which was barred on the inside. He removed the bar, opened the door, and then stopped dead in his tracks. Dack Hoose was standing ten feet out in the yard in the glaring sunlight, holding a double-barrelled shotgun in his hands which lifted instantly to point its deadly twin muzzles directly at Harper's chest.

3

Hoose waggled the twin muzzles of the shotgun, his face contorted with menace. 'Throw up your hands!' He spoke thickly. 'Where's Fargo?'

'If you're talking about the man who was shooting at me — he's dead,' Harper replied. 'Put down the gun, Hoose. You're in enough trouble already without adding to it by obstructing me.'

'Don't tell me what to do. In case you haven't noticed, you're on the wrong end of this gun. And I ain't got any trouble, so what are you cooking up now? I run my business with no trouble, and I ain't gonna be dragged into anything.'

'It looks like you're mixed up in something,' Harper said grimly. 'I reckon you're in cahoots with the man I just killed. You called him Fargo. How did you know he was in the barn if he turned up in the night while you were asleep?

'You killed him?' Hoose thumbed back the hammers on the shotgun. He snickered, his narrowed eyes glinting. 'You're the one in big trouble right now, Harper. I'm gonna fill you with buckshot. This gun will make a helluva hole in your brisket at this range.'

Harper studied Hoose, wondering what was in the man's mind. There was no way he could regain the initiative over him while he was standing ten yards away and holding a levelled shotgun. He was puzzled by Hoose's reason for confronting him.

'You wouldn't hold me up without a good reason, Hoose,' he persisted, 'so what's on your mind? What have you got yourself mixed up in?'

'Nothing, I tell you! You're always sneaking around here trying to make out that I'm living on the wrong side of the law, and I'm way past my gills with it. I'm gonna stop you coming again, and then maybe I'll get some peace.'

'You're not making sense.' Harper shook his head. 'I've never accused you of any wrongdoing. All I've ever done is drop by to ask if you've seen rustled cattle going by, or any outlaws a posse has been after. I ask the same questions of all the ranchers in the county, and they don't get riled up by it. They're only too pleased to help the law.'

Hoose motioned with the shotgun. 'Go round to the back of the barn. I'm gonna let you have it. No one will ever know you were here. I'll bury you deep and run horse tracks over your grave.'

Harper caught a glimpse of movement on the range beyond the far end of the barn, and saw a rider coming in fast. The horse looked familiar, and he experienced a thrill of hope when he recognized the animal as his buckskin, which Lily-Beth had been riding. The rider drew nearer and hoofbeats drummed the hard ground. Hoose heard the sound and began to turn his head to check who was arriving, but he realized that Harper's pistol was still in its holster, so

53

he forced down his curiosity and lifted the shotgun a fraction. Harper recognized the rider as Lily-Beth, and she was holding a pistol in her right hand.

'You are in bad trouble now,' Harper observed, then bluffed: 'Here's one of my posse men coming in. If you turn around I'll get you, and if my man sees you covering me with a shotgun he'll shoot you without hesitation. You'd better put the gun down, Hoose, and be pretty damn quick about it.'

Hoose's face expressed indecision. He could hear the approaching rider's hoofs but dared not take his eyes off Harper. Then his nerve failed him; he cursed and threw down the shotgun. Harper drew his pistol and cocked it.

Lily-Beth came into the yard, reined in and almost fell out of the saddle. Harper saw signs of distress in the girl's face and hurried past Hoose, slamming his gun barrel against the trader's skull as he went by. Hoose groaned and dropped to the ground. Harper bent and searched the man for other weapons, found none, and picked up the shotgun, which he hurled across the yard. The next instant Lily-Beth was in his arms, her face buried against his broad chest. She sobbed unrestrainedly.

Harper looked around, wondering whether the girl was being followed, but the range was silent and still. He looked at Hoose, crumpled in the dust. The trader was beginning to stir. Harper transferred his pistol to his left hand and used his right to lift Lily-Beth's chin. He looked searchingly into her strained face. Her eyes were brimming with tears. She was trembling uncontrollably and exhibiting shock in every line of countenance.

'What happened, Lily?' Harper demanded. 'Where's the rider who took you from the ranch last night? I've been following your tracks since first light.'

'I think I've killed him,' she said raggedly, her breathing laboured. 'It has been like a nightmare, Brad. When I left you at the ranch last night to wait by the stream I almost rode down the man who took me away. He was waiting just clear of the ranch, and told me he would take me to Bob. I was forced to go along with him, and we rode all night. Later we were joined by another rider, a bearded man who wanted to kill me, but the first man said I was needed to sign the ranch over to them.'

Harper frowned as he listened, wondering what was coming next. Lily-Beth gulped and blinked away her tears.

'What was Hoose doing pointing a shotgun at you?' she demanded.

'Don't worry about Hoose,' he replied. 'We'll be taking him to jail. What happened with the man who took you last night?'

'He was against killing me out of hand. I was terrified, Brad. I was told that Bob had been taken prisoner on the range and they wanted him to sign over the ranch to them, but Bob wouldn't do it so they came for me. They reckoned Bob would sign if he saw me in trouble. I said I wouldn't sign anything, no matter what they did. I told them you would be trailing me as soon as daylight came, and you had a half-share in the ranch so no one could sign anything over without your say-so. The bearded man said he'd come back here and wait for you to show up.'

'He was waiting,' Harper said, 'and I ain't crying because I had to kill him.' He was watching Hoose intently and saw the trader begin to stir. 'Stay down, Hoose, or I'll shoot you in the leg,' he called.

Hoose looked around, saw the gun in Harper's hand, and relaxed.

'So how did you get away from the man holding you?' Harper demanded.

'He made me cook breakfast,' Lily-Beth replied. 'He was sitting on his bedroll beside the fire smoking a cigarette while I made coffee. When the water had boiled I tossed it in his face and snatched his pistol. He came at me to grab the gun, missed, and fell against me. The gun went off accidentally and the bullet hit him in the chest. It was awful, Brad. He fell down with blood spilling everywhere. I jumped on your horse and fled. I knew you'd be out trailing the buckskin so I rode along my back trail.'

'You did well, Lily,' Harper commented. 'I was in a spot of bother here and you saved me when you rode in. Forget about the man who took you. He was playing some deep game and lost out. We have to concern ourselves about the spot Bob is in. It seems like the two men who could lead us to him are dead so let us hope Hoose knows something. I think he's mixed up in this, I'll try and make him tell me what he knows. Take a look in the buckskin's saddle-bags. I carry a pair of handcuffs. Let's make Hoose helpless and then I'll get to work on him.'

He released Lily-Beth and the girl fetched the handcuffs from the buckskin. Harper put the cuffs on Hoose's wrists, and the trader began to object vociferously.

'You got nothing on me,' he snarled.

58

'I wasn't going to shoot you, Harper. What do you take me for? I wouldn't step out of line against the law.'

'Button your lip,' Harper told him. 'You'll get your chance to talk when I'm ready to listen. Right now I could do with a stiff drink and some breakfast. After that you can talk, and you better give me straight answers or you'll be real sorry I crossed your trail. There's something mighty bad going on around the county and I want to put a stop to it but quick. I guess you're mixed up in it, Hoose, and I'm gonna get to the bottom of it before I'm done.'

'We've got to get on Bob's trail.' Lily-Beth's voice quivered as she spoke, and Harper could see that the girl was under great strain. He nodded sympathetically.

'I sure wish I could be in several places at once,' he replied, 'but as that ain't possible I'm gonna have to decide what should be handled first. I reckon it is gonna be a long haul to find Bob and yank him out of the trouble he's in, so we'd better prepare ourselves and get into the best possible condition to do what may be required of us. Let's go see what Hoose has got in the way of supplies, huh?'

He prodded Hoose with his pistol and followed the man into the trading post. He unfastened the cuff around Hoose's left wrist to snap it shut around a metal rail on the edge of the bar. Lily-Beth went through to the living-quarters at the rear of the store and started to prepare breakfast. Harper faced Hoose.

'OK.' he said. 'You can start talking now, and don't forget what I said about telling the truth.'

'I don't know anything,' Hoose growled. 'What the hell would I know about the goings-on in the county while I'm stuck out here in the middle of nowhere? Some days I don't see even one rider passing through.'

'That man I killed out in the barn: you named him as Fargo, yet as far as I can tell you didn't know he was out there. So what kind of an arrangement did you have with him? He shot at me without a challenge. I reckon you saw me riding in from way off and warned him I was coming because he'd told you he wanted to get me and was expecting me to show up looking for Lily-Beth.'

'You've got me all wrong, Harper. Sure, I knew he was in my barn. He rode in just before you did, and said he expected you to trail through today. Don't ask me how he knew that, but that's what he said. He told me he'd gut-shoot me if I didn't go along with his plans, and I told him it was none of my business what he got up to. I'm alone out here and I never stick my nose in anything that don't concern me, nor ask for trouble.'

Harper studied Hoose's face but could not tell whether the trader was on the level. Lily-Beth had said she told her captors that she expected him to trail after her, so it was likely Hoose was telling the truth.

'I'm gonna believe you just this once, Hoose,' Harper decided. 'You could be telling the truth, and I ain't gonna waste time flogging a dead horse.'

'Are you gonna turn me loose?' Hoose's expression cleared and he grinned.

'The hell I am! I'm gonna take you into Clear Spring and let the sheriff handle you. He'll keep you behind bars until he's satisfied with your story.'

'Hell! What about my business? I need to be here day and night or I'll be robbed blind. You can't do this to me, Harper. You can leave me here, and I'll still be on the spot when you get back. I ain't going any place.'

'No dice! Bob Fuller is in the hands of some bad men and I've got to go look for him. I don't want you loose on my back trail. You were ready to blast me with that shotgun, and yet you say you're not mixed up in anything. So you'll stay under arrest until I find out what is going on.'

Hoose protested but Harper was not

listening. Hoose protested further when Harper poured himself a shot of whiskey and gulped it.

'I hope you're gonna pay for that,' Hoose said hopefully. 'And the breakfast that gal is cooking ain't for free. I'm running a business here.'

'You'll get everything that is owing to you,' Harper said thinly.

Lily-Beth peered out of the kitchen doorway, wiping her hands on a cloth. A strand of blonde hair hung over her left eye and she thrust it back off her face.

'Brad, I can hear riders out back,' she said. Her face was set in a stiff expression and fear shone in her blue eyes.

Harper drew his pistol and ran past her to a window in the kitchen that overlooked the back yard. He saw two riders reining in before the open door of the barn. One of the men dismounted and went into the barn. The other remained in his saddle, his hand on the butt of his holstered pistol; he was fully alert as he looked around. Harper remained out of view, watching intently. The man in the barn reappeared in the doorway.

'Hey, Skinny, Fargo is dead in here. He's been shot.'

'The hell you say!' Skinny replied. 'I always said we couldn't trust Hoose. Pendle knew him in Wichita and said he couldn't be relied on. Let's grab him, Carney, and find out what happened.'

Both men drew their pistols and led their horses across the yard to the kitchen door. Harper moved forward, gun ready. As Skinny opened the door Harper lunged forward, striking at the man's gun hand with the long barrel of his pistol. Skinny yelped in pain and dropped his gun. Harper placed his left hand against the man's chest and thrust him backwards, off balance. Skinny collided with his companion and they both fell to the ground. A gun fired, sending heavy echoes across the yard. Skinny yelled in sudden pain and slumped limply on top of his sidekick.

64

Harper followed up quickly. He kicked at the pistol the second man was holding and it dropped into the dust. He continued forward, kicking the gun clear.

'Get up and do it slow,' Harper ordered.

The two men were lying together and Harper saw blood staining Skinny's shirt about waist high. Carney thrust off his companion and got to his feet. He was badly shocked, and stood looking down at the injured man.

'Throw up your hands,' Harper ordered.

'He fell against me and my gun went off,' Carney said, shaking his head.

'What were you doing with drawn guns?' Harper countered. 'Were you planning to shoot someone? What's your name and what do you want here?'

'I'm Bill Carney. We were looking for our pard Fargo, and I found him lying dead in the barn. We reckoned to ask Hoose what happened.'

'I killed Fargo,' Harper said. 'He shot at me without warning. He was your pard, huh? So tell me what is going on around here? Fargo was with another man who abducted a girl from the Bar F ranch last night, and he stopped off here to catch me when I rode in. Talk, Carney, and give me the truth.'

Carney was gazing at the law star on Harper's shirt front as if he had never seen one before. Skinny was motionless; his eyes were closed and he was groaning. The bloodstain on his shirt had widened.

'What's Skinny's name?' Harper demanded.

'Cal Johnson.'

'You'd better take a look at him. I want him alive.'

Carney dropped to his knees beside Johnson and rolled him over. Harper saw that the bullet had struck the man in the small of the back.

'Do what you can to stop the bleeding,' Harper suggested. 'Patch him up and we'll leave him here. I'll take you to jail and send the doctor out to tend him.'

Lily-Beth came to Harper's side. 'Brad, I can hear riders coming from the direction of town,' she said worriedly.

Harper clenched his teeth. 'Carney,' he rapped. 'Come with me and be quick. I've got some more company coming in.'

Carney got to his feet and entered the kitchen. Harper thrust the muzzle of his pistol against the man's side.

'Lie down on the floor over by that window so I can keep an eye on you,' Harper said.

He waited until the man had obeyed, then crossed to the door. He glanced back at the impassive Hoose, then eased the door open a fraction to peer out. Two riders were coming in at a canter; relief filled him when he recognized them as two of the townsmen who usually turned out when a posse was required.

'It's Joe Hilliard and Tom Caton,' he announced. 'I reckon the sheriff must be worried about what's going on, and I could sure do with some help.'

He motioned for Carney to join him and pushed the man outside as the two riders came up. Hilliard, a carpenter, was tall and broad, with blue eyes and a shock of blond hair showing under the brim of his hat. He was in his early twenties, and had an angular face that was never without a smile. Caton was much older. He worked for Denton, the undertaker in Clear Spring, and the nature of his work had made him serious-minded and reticent.

'Howdy, Brad,' Hilliard greeted. 'Mort sent us to keep an eye on you.'

'He did right this time,' Harper replied. 'Have you got some handcuffs with you?'

'Sure have!' Hilliard dismounted, rummaged in a saddle-bag, and produced a pair of handcuffs. 'Are we in time for some breakfast? Whatever is cooking sure smells good.'

'You can help yourselves,' Harper said. 'Put the cuffs on this guy. His name is Bill Carney. Two of his pards are out back. One is dead in the barn and the other was shot accidentally. There's a third man out on the trail somewhere, and I expect he's dead.'

'Jeez! What happened?' Hilliard's expression sobered quickly. 'So that's why we were sent out! The law department was expecting trouble. What's going on, Brad? Are we in time for some action?'

'I didn't know what to expect,' Harper replied, 'and I've got a pretty good notion that the trouble hasn't really started yet. Keep an eye on Carney. You can take him and Hoose back to town and tell Mort to hold them until I get back. Do you think you can handle that chore?'

Hilliard nodded. He snapped the cuffs on Carney's wrists and pushed him back into the trading post. Hoose started whining about being innocent, and Hilliard threatened him into silence. Harper turned to Lily-Beth, who was standing in the doorway to the kitchen. She was trembling and seemed exhausted.

'Let's have some breakfast and coffee,' Harper suggested. 'It'll be a long day, Lily. I want to set eyes on Bob before sundown so we'd better get moving.'

Lily-Beth nodded and turned back into the kitchen, thankful for something to occupy her mind. Harper took a plate of bacon and bread from her and began to eat ravenously. His experience in law dealing had made him aware that one ate when one found the opportunity, for on the trail there was no telling where the next meal would come from. He cleared the plate and drank two cups of coffee, insisted that Lily ate, then sacked up supplies to take along with them.

'I'm in a hurry, Tom,' Harper told Hilliard. 'You know what to do, so get busy when you've eaten. Tell the sheriff I have Lily-Beth with me and I'm still following tracks. Don't lose your prisoners, huh?'

'They'll be in jail when you get back to town,' Hilliard replied.

70

Harper led Lily-Beth out to the back yard and helped her into the saddle of one of the horses standing there. He mounted his buckskin and they rode out fast. Lily's tracks were plain and he led the way at a fast canter. His thoughts were muddled as he tried to make sense out of what had occurred. There seemed to be at least a dozen strangers in the county who were ready to kill for what they wanted. They had attacked Bar F, captured Bob Fuller, and tried to get Bob to sign away his rights to the ranch. They had told Lily she would be killed. And one of the two men who had ridden into the trading post had mentioned someone called Pendle who had known Hoose back in Wichita.

'Brad, that man I shot is lying just over that crest to the left,' Lily said eventually.

Harper changed direction immediately. He reined in swiftly when he reached the crest and saw a motionless figure beyond it, huddled in the grass.

'Stay back, Lily,' Harper said, and she reined in thankfully.

Harper dismounted and approached the man, a stranger, and saw at a glance that he was dead. A large bloodstain covered the front of his shirt — the bullet which killed him had struck the centre of his chest. Harper shook his head and turned his attention to the man's horse, which was grazing nearby. He searched the saddlebags, looking for identification, but found nothing, so he returned to the dead man to empty his pockets. He found only those small anonymous items which most men carried on the trail.

'Is he dead?' Lily-Beth called.

'He couldn't be any deader!' Harper replied. 'Don't worry about it, Lily. Just concentrate on Bob. We've got to find him pretty damn quick. I've run out of tracks now so we're gonna have to try and work out where this guy was taking you. Did he say anything while you were in his company which could pinpoint where he was heading?'

'I don't recall anything. He was close-mouthed; said I would be killed if I didn't do like he said. All he did say was that they had Bob and he was being difficult.'

'At least we know Bob is still alive,' Harper mused. He considered the general direction they had travelled, and in his mind's eye saw the range ahead in the same direction. 'There's only the AH ranch ahead of us,' he said, thinking aloud, and shaking his head. 'I can't believe Abe Hickman would be involved in this business, but I guess we'll have to check him out. He did show up at your place last night just after the fire was started.'

Lily-Beth rode up beside Harper, trying to keep her gaze averted from the dead man. Her face was pale and her expression suggested that she was living in a nightmare.

'There's that deserted spread on Antelope Creek, Brad,' she said. 'We could have been heading there.'

'That was Dan Benton's ranch!'

Harper grimaced. 'It's been about three years now since old Benton died. There was talk a year or so ago that Benton's nephew was coming to take it over, but so far he ain't showed up. Maybe you've hit on something, Lily. This crooked bunch is more likely to be holed up on a deserted ranch than using a spread like AH. Hickman has got more than a dozen riders on his payroll, and word would get out mighty quick if any thing bad was happening there.'

'Brad, don't look now,' Lily-Beth said worriedly, 'but there's a rider watching us on a rise to your right. Ah, he's eased back out of sight now! We'd better be careful and get off the skyline.'

Harper did not hesitate. He grasped Lily-Beth's reins and led her back over the rise. Just before they reached cover a bullet crackled over their heads and the report of a rifle shot smashed the heavy silence.

4

Harper dismounted hurriedly, calling for Lily-Beth to take cover as he snatched his rifle from its scabbard. He dropped to the ground, crawled forward to the crest, and removed his Stetson before taking a quick look at the ground beyond. He saw nothing, and settled down to watch the apparently deserted rangeland. There was no movement out there, and although he could still hear faint gun echoes in the vast distance of the illimitable range there was a heavy, ominous silence around him which added to the tensions of the moment.

Lily-Beth crawled to Harper's side and he glanced at her, shaking his head.

'I don't see a thing,' he said. 'But someone fired that shot at us and it could only be one of those men who took Bob. If I were alone I'd hunt him down, but I can't take any chances with you along, Lily. I wish now that I'd arranged for Joe Hilliard to take you back to town, but I don't want to let you out of my sight. If we remain together then anyone wanting to grab you will have to go through me.'

'You couldn't shake me off, Brad,' Lily-Beth said with an edge of determination. 'We must find Bob before those men decide to kill him.'

'I don't think we have to worry about Bob's life.' Harper returned his gaze to the range ahead. 'If they want him to sign over Bar F, then while he refuses to do so they'll keep him alive. Let's just hope he can hold out.'

'I think we should have headed back to our range instead of riding out this way,' Lily-Beth mused. 'You could have picked up Bob's tracks and trailed him without trouble.'

'I'm sure we're going in the right direction, so I'll keep pushing on.' Harper eased back from the crest. 'You drop back and follow me at a distance. I don't want you to ride into another ambush. Just keep me in sight and we'll get along fine.'

Lily-Beth did not reply but her expression showed that she did not like his instructions. Harper shook his head as he swung into his saddle. He kept his Winchester in his left hand as he rode on, and when he glanced over his shoulder he saw Lily-Beth dropping back. He pushed on at a canter, making for the ridge where Lily-Beth had seen the figure, but when he reached the spot there was no sign of the man, although he saw tracks in the long grass.

The hoofprints led in the general direction of Antelope Creek and Harper pushed on. He was beyond trying to make sense out of what had occurred and decided to confront events as and when they developed. He kept an eye on Lily-Beth, toiling along behind, and the sight of the girl on his back trail only served to make him aware of the grim reality of the situation.

It was past noon when he topped a rise and saw Antelope Creek. He rode quickly back into cover when he saw horses and men around the small cattle ranch beside the creek. He dismounted, crawled forward to observe, and counted five men lounging around the small frame house. There were a dozen saddle mounts in a pole corral, and a small barn was off to the right, where a man with a rifle was lounging in the doorway on lookout.

Lily-Beth came up, dismounted, and crawled beside Harper to peer down at the ranch.

'Well, what about that?' she exclaimed. 'When I was out this way about a month ago there was no one around; the place was deserted. Now it looks like it is being run as a cattle spread again. Do you reckon Dan Benton's nephew turned up to claim it?'

'I don't see any steers around.' Harper shook his head. 'Take a look at the horses in that corral. Do you see Bob's mount down there?'

Lily-Beth subjected the corral to an intense scrutiny, and then gave a low cry.

'That's his sorrel in there. I'd know it anywhere, Brad. What can we do?'

'What we can't do is ride in there openly and ask to see Bob,' Harper replied. 'I'll wait until sundown and then sneak in for a look-see. If Bob is in there I'll get him out.'

'But that's hours away,' Lily-Beth protested, 'and there's no telling what they might do to Bob in the meantime. There are five men down there, Brad, and you should be able to get the drop on them. We can't just sit around out here while they may be torturing Bob. I'll cover you with a rifle, and if they start anything I'll join in. I won't be squeamish about shooting any of them.'

Harper shook his head. 'I'll only get one chance at busting Bob out of there, so I ain't going off half-cocked,' he said sharply. 'Take a hold on your patience, Lily, and let me do this right. There's a lot at stake here, and we're playing with

79

Bob's life. These men have shown that they are cold-blooded killers, and I can't afford to take any chances with them.'

Lily-Beth subsided, her face twisted with mingled hope and despair. 'You're right,' she said softly. 'Play it how you think it should be done, Brad. But I just hope you get it right.'

Harper did not reply. He studied the ranch below, looking for a likely approach under the cover of darkness. When he saw two men leave the house and head for the corral he nudged Lily-Beth. The girl's eyes glittered like a wildcat's when she saw the men saddling their mounts.

'They're gonna ride out,' she mused. 'I'll follow them and see what they get up to.'

'Are you loco?' Harper gazed at her in amazement. 'After what you've been through, do you still want to take a chance of falling into their hands? Heck. I'm bending over backwards trying to keep you out of trouble, so don't make matters worse for me. Just stay in the background and keep your head down if lead starts flying.'

He could tell by Lily-Beth's expression that she was not enamoured of his attitude. She picked up his Winchester and checked the weapon expertly.

'You won't need this at close quarters, and I want to be able to defend myself when you get busy down there,' she said defiantly.

Harper tried to snatch the gun from her but she slid away, shaking her head. He suppressed a sigh and returned to checking out the approach to the ranch. He saw the two men at the corral swing into their saddles and ride out to the east. He kept his eyes on them until they disappeared over a ridge beyond the ranch house. Then he dismissed them from his mind. As far as he could tell there were now just three men left to oppose him, but he would have to move in immediately, before the situation changed.

'Stay here by the horses,' he said.

Lily-Beth nodded. 'I need a clear mind when I get down there, so just lie low, huh?'

'You're not going to wait until sundown?' she queried, and her expression showed relief when he shook his head.

'I want Bob out of there as much as you do,' he said. 'Whatever happens, don't reveal yourself. If it goes badly for me then ride hell for leather to Clear Spring and report to the sheriff. Bland needs to know what is going on out here.'

Lily-Beth nodded. 'Take care, Brad, and good luck,' she said softly.

Harper smiled. 'Luck doesn't come into it,' he replied.

He checked his pistol and slipped away, moving into a gully that would cover his approach most of the way to the ranch house. He glanced back once to see Lily-Beth watching him with his rifle clutched in her hands, her face contorted by worry. He continued resolutely, relieved now that the time for action had arrived. All of his attention was concentrated on what he had to do.

The ranch house lay only fifty yards ahead when Harper reached the spot just outside the yard where the gully petered out. He drew his pistol and looked for a way to get to the rear of the house without being seen. Two men were sitting on the porch of the house; he wondered what the third man was doing. He eased out of the gully and crawled across open ground to the right, watching the two men on the porch intently for the first sign that he had been spotted. But he reached the side of the house without raising an outcry and he paused for some moments, steeling himself for what had to be done next.

There were two men outside the house and, as far as he knew, only one man inside, so he was aware of what he had to do. He edged along the side of the house to the rear corner and peered around it. The barn with its open door was across the back yard and he studied the area for several moments. Nothing moved over there, although he had seen a guard when he first observed the lay-out. He switched his gaze to the back of the house. The kitchen door was ajar, he noted; he moved towards it with his gun levelled. He made no sound as he looked into the kitchen, which was empty. An inner door stood half open, which enabled him to look along a passage to the big front room overlooking the porch.

There was no sound inside the house. Harper eased out of the kitchen and looked around. There were doors on either side of the passage, and he was about to move in to check them when he heard a cry of pain which seemed to come from the upper storey of the building. He paused when the cry sounded again, then he ascended the stairs in a hurry. He halted in an upper passage that stretched the whole length of the house. Several doors gave access to bedrooms, and they were all ajar. Again he heard a cry of pain, and cocked his pistol as he eased towards the sound.

'Why don't you make it easy on yourself?' a harsh voice demanded from inside the room that Harper was approaching. 'You'll do what you're told in the end so you could save yourself a lot of pain by signing right now.'

'Go to hell!' a man replied, and Harper recognized Bob Fuller's voice. 'You'll kill me before you get me to sign anything. You're wasting your time, mister.'

'We've got plenty of time, Fuller, and you'll do what we want before you're through.'

Harper pushed open the door of the room and halted in shock when he saw Bob Fuller, stripped to the waist and tied to an iron-framed bed with his wrists and ankles lashed to the bed posts. A man was bending over Bob with a hunting knife in his hand, and was digging the point of the blade into the flesh of Fuller's left shoulder. Harper lunged forward, swinging his gun barrel, and laid the weapon solidly against the man's head. He grasped the man with his left hand as he collapsed, and lowered him to the floor. The man struggled to resist and Harper slugged him again with considerable force. The man jerked and relaxed inertly beside the bed. Harper picked up the discarded knife and straightened to turn his attention to Bob Fuller.

'What have you got yourself into, Bob?' Harper demanded as he cut the rope binding his friend. Fuller's upper chest was covered with more than a dozen cuts, his face was badly bruised, his left eye completely closed, and his cheeks carried the dull red marks of violence.

'Brad, am I glad to see you?' Fuller muttered. 'I knew you would come for me but it sure took you a hell of a time. I don't think I could have held out much longer. That's Frank Benton you've put down. He's a nephew of old

Dan Benton. From what I've over-heard, he took over this place last week, and he sure brought a bad bunch of riders with him. They caused all that trouble east of here that we heard so much about last year, and now they've set up business in this county. There are at least a dozen of them, and they plan a big take-over on the range.'

Harper bent over Benton and removed a pistol from a low-slung holster. He tossed the weapon on to the bed beside Fuller.

'I hope you can ride, Bob,' he said. 'We're getting out of here pronto. I'll hogtie this cuss. There are two men sitting on the porch, and I don't want to bring them into a fight right now because I've got Lily-Beth waiting for us back of a ridge and I don't like her to be left alone too long. She was taken last night by a couple of these men, but she killed one of them and got away. Come on, rattle your hocks and see if you can stand.'

Fuller groaned as he pushed himself

to his feet. He staggered, and Harper grasped his arm to steady him. Fuller thrust off Harper's hand and picked up the pistol lying on the bed. Blood was smearing his chest but he picked up his shirt and groaned as he pulled it on.

'I'm well enough to want some satisfaction from these men,' he growled. 'Let's take those two on the porch before we do anything else. We're gonna have to kill them before this trouble ends, so let's do it now, while we have an edge.'

'I need to get you to town to make a report to the sheriff on what's been happening, Bob.' Harper tied Frank Benton with the rope he had removed from Fuller. 'A posse will turn out for these men.'

'And they'll be long gone before you can get back for them,' Fuller protested. 'Come on, Brad, let's do this right.'

Before Harper could reply a harsh voice called up the stairs from the ground floor.

'Hey, Frank, get down here right now, huh? That deputy from town is riding in. You better come and talk to him.'

Harper frowned. 'What deputy from town?'

'He ain't talking about you,' Fuller said, buttoning his shirt with some difficulty, 'and Joss Kemp is the only other deputy in the county. So what in hell is he doing out here? Do you think he knows what is going on?'

'Nothing would surprise me where Kemp is concerned,' Harper replied. 'Let's go down and join the party.'

'Now you're talking!' Fuller checked the pistol.

'Just back me up,' Harper advised. 'I'll play it according to the book.'

He left the room and hastened to the stairs, his boots sounding loud on the uncarpeted wooden floor. Fuller followed closely. Harper descended the stairs and headed for the front room overlooking the yard. One of the men who had been lounging on the porch when Harper arrived was standing in the doorway looking out across the yard. He heard Harper's feet on the boards, glanced over his shoulder, then did a double-take as his mind registered the fact that Harper was a stranger.

'What the hell?' he exclaimed, dropping his right hand to his holstered six-gun.

'Get your hands up,' Harper called, cocking his pistol.

The man hesitated before lifting his hands shoulder high. He gazed at Harper in amazement.

'Come in out of the doorway,' Harper ordered, and the man moved quickly to comply. Harper went forward and snatched the pistol out of the man's holster. He thrust the man towards Bob Fuller, who stuck the muzzle of the gun he was holding against the man's chest. 'Keep him quiet, Bob,' Harper said.

Harper peered out of the door and saw Joss Kemp riding in across the yard. The man on the porch was leaning against a post, watching Kemp's approach. Harper stayed back out of sight, suspicion of Kemp flaring in his mind when he saw

Kemp's easy manner; he realized that the next few moments would either settle his doubts or prove Kemp's duplicity.

'Howdy,' Kemp called as he reined in before the porch. 'Is Frank around? I got some bad news for him. I came by the trading post and there's been bad trouble there. A couple of posse men had Hoose under arrest along with one of your men. Brad Harper, the chief deputy, showed up there and killed a couple of your men. The Fuller gal was being brought here but she escaped and joined Harper, so it looks like your plan is busted.'

'The hell you say!' The man on the porch turned to the door and called loudly. 'Hey, Frank, where the hell are you? Get out here and talk to Kemp.'

'But it ain't as bad as it sounds,' Kemp added. 'I killed the two posse men and turned Hoose and your man loose. But you'll have to take care of Harper because he is hell on wheels, and he'll spoil your game if you give him half a chance. I've had the feeling for some time that he's wise to me, so you better put him out of it fast.'

Harper fought down his shock at Kemp's revelation. He stepped out to the porch with his pistol levelled. Kemp was in the act of dismounting, but caught Harper's movement in the doorway and turned with an easy smile on his lips, expecting to see Frank Benton. His expression changed quickly when he recognized Harper. His reaction was to reach for his holstered pistol in a fast draw.

Harper fired swiftly, aiming for Kemp's upper chest. The blasting shot tore the heavy silence asunder and echoes fled as gun smoke flew. The .45 slug smacked into Kemp's chest, he jerked and lost all interest in his gun. The weapon was only half-drawn when he crumpled into the dust of the yard. Harper's gaze flickered to the man on the porch, who was staring at him in astonishment, his mouth agape in shock.

'Get your hands up,' Harper rapped.

The man obeyed instantly.

Harper took the man's pistol, then stepped off the porch to approach Kemp, who was semi-conscious and groaning. Harper took Kemp's pistol and stuck it into the waistband of his pants. He bent and examined the deputy, saw that the wound was high in the chest, and figured that Kemp would survive to answer questions. Kemp's eyes opened and he gazed up at Harper.

'What the hell were you doing inside the house?' he demanded. 'I might have known you'd be around. I guess you overheard what I said about Hilliard and Caton, huh?'

'Did you kill them?' Harper demanded.

'What else?' Kemp shook his head in disbelief at the turn of events.

Bob Fuller escorted his prisoner out to the porch. 'I heard what you said, Kemp, you four-flusher,' he grated, 'and I'll have great pleasure giving evidence against you. You're as bad as the rest of these prairie wolves. Take that badge off him, Brad; he ain't fit to wear it.'

93

'Let's bind these two.' Harper removed Kemp's deputy's star. 'How are you feeling, Bob? Are you up to the trip to town? Right now you look like you're ready to drop.'

'I'll see these buzzards into the jail,' Fuller replied. 'Where is Lily-Beth? She shouldn't be out here alone.'

'We'll pick her up on the way out. Get that rope off Kemp's horse and tie these two, then I'll get horses for them while you watch them. The sooner we get out of here the better.'

'Now I've got a gun in my hand the rest of this bunch can turn up any time they please,' Fuller said. 'Is Kemp able to sit a horse?'

'He'll ride into town or die on the way,' Harper responded.

He was impatient now to get back to Lily-Beth and hastened his preparations. The two prisoners were bound. Harper fetched Frank Benton down from the bedroom and left Fuller watching the hapless trio while he went to the corral and saddled horses. They were loading the prisoners on to mounts when Harper heard the sound of approaching hoofs and looked across the yard to see Lily-Beth riding in, leading his horse.

'Brad, there are two riders coming this way from Clear Spring,' the girl called. 'I thought you'd better know about them; they could bring more trouble. I see you've freed Bob.'

'I'm sure glad to see you, Lily-Beth!' Fuller grinned at his sister. 'Brad told me you had some trouble with this crooked bunch. Don't dismount. We're about ready to ride.'

Harper was linking together the reins of the horses which the prisoners were riding. Kemp was semi-conscious and unbound. He sat slumped in his saddle. His shirt was soaked to the waist with blood. Harper felt no sympathy for the man. He turned his attention to Fuller, who groaned when he swung into his saddle.

'Do you think you can make it, Bob?' he queried.

'I'd die trying,' Fuller replied. He straightened in his saddle and covered the prisoners with his pistol. 'Let's get out of here. I've spent long enough here to last me a lifetime.'

'I want to see who is coming in,' Harper said. 'Take this bunch around to the back of the house and keep them quiet. I'll wait on the porch for the riders and check them out.'

Fuller grinned. 'You better take off your law badge, then, or you'll spoil your play. No doubt they will be more of Benton's bad guys.'

Harper nodded and removed his star as Fuller led the prisoners out of sight. He spotted two riders approaching and reloaded his pistol. The newcomers cantered into the yard, the hoofs of their mounts kicking up dust. They were strangers to Harper, who stood motionless, watching them intently, his right hand down at his side.

The men were dressed in store suits. Harper eyed them critically as they reined in before him. One man was old, probably in his early fifties, clean-shaven and sharp-eyed. He was fleshy, his round face sagging around the jowls. His mouth was just a thin straight line under his large nose. He was wearing a gunbelt with a pistol in a low-slung holster. His blue suit looked expensive. His riding-boots were made of hand-tooled leather, as was his saddle. The second man was twenty years younger, wearing a brown suit made of cheap material. He was not wearing a gunbelt but there was a significant bulge in the region of his left armpit. He was tall and lean, his face angular, with dark eyes bearing a keen light as if he were poised on a knife-edge and perpetually ready for action.

'Howdy?' Harper greeted. 'Riding through?'

'We got business with Frank Benton,' the older man said. 'Is he around?'

'He ain't right now.' Harper leaned his left shoulder against an awning post. 'He left me in the big saddle here, so how can I help you?'

'I'm Norton Calder,' the older man introduced himself. 'I own the sawmill that's just opened up in Clear Spring. I understand that Benton has purchased the Fuller ranch and needs a new house built there. I can supply his wants promptly and cheaply. Do you expect him back soon? I could wait for his return.'

'I don't think he'll be back before tomorrow morning,' Harper replied. 'There was a shooting at the trading post involving some of our crew and Frank has gone to sort it out.'

'You've had some trouble here,' the younger man observed in a low, fierce tone. 'There's blood in the dust. Looks like someone got badly hurt.'

'Someone is always getting hurt around here,' Harper said harshly. 'A guy stepped out of line. That's the kind of outfit we are.'

'I've seen you before somewhere,' the younger man continued in a harsher tone. 'I never forget a face, and I sure saw yours recently. Now where was it?' He paused, his dark eyes narrowed. 'Yeah — Clear Spring yesterday. I saw you coming out of the sheriff's office, and you were wearing a deputy badge then.' His right hand began to edge across his chest to where his gun was holstered under his left armpit.

'Lay off him, Badger,' Calder said sharply. 'He doesn't look like a man who can take a joke. Benton told me last week he had a local deputy in his back pocket. So this must be him. What's your name, Deputy?'

'Joss Kemp,' Harper replied.

'The hell you are!' Badger retorted. 'I know Kemp. I was drinking in the saloon in town with him last night, and as there are only two deputies in town you must be the other one. Kemp said to watch out for you.'

'What's it to you who I am if you are a law-abiding man?' Harper demanded. 'You'd better ride out of here if you're not looking for trouble. I'll tell Frank you called, but as far as I know the

Fuller ranch ain't his yet. He's having a mite of trouble swinging the deal.'

'I ain't satisfied with this galoot's gab.' Badger's right hand was edging inside his jacket, and Harper, watching him intently, slid his fingers around the butt of his holstered pistol.

'You better change your mind about reaching for your gun,' Harper warned.

'Badger, I told you to lay off,' Calder said in a rising tone. 'Our business ain't urgent, and I can see Benton later. Come on, let's head back to town.'

'I don't think Benton went to the trading post,' Badger said. 'I reckon he's in trouble here. This deal has got a bad smell about it. We better take a look around because we'll get trouble from Stross if we don't check this out.'

Harper tensed as Badger continued to slide his right hand under his jacket. Calder remained silent but dropped his hand to his holster. The silence suddenly acquired an air of hostility, and the next instant harsh reality exploded as Badger made a fast draw from his shoulder holster. Harper went into action simultaneously, drawing his gun and cocking it in one fluid motion, and then shooting erupted deafeningly . . .

5

Harper lifted his pistol. Out of the corner of his eye he saw Calder pulling his gun, but Badger was fast, and a split second ahead of Harper, who realized the fact in the instant before he brought his muzzle to bear on the man. He threw himself to the left in a desperate attempt to put Badger off aim, and crashed to the porch on his left side even as he fired. Badger got off his shot first and the slug tore a long splinter out of the porch a scant inch from Harper's left hip. Then Badger jerked under the impact of a hit and dropped his pistol instantly. He twisted in his saddle, trying desperately to remain in leather.

Calder brought his gun into action, but he was agitated and his shot struck the wall just above Harper, who jerked his gun hand around and fired a quick shot in Calder's direction. Calder dropped his gun and hauled on his reins to kick his horse into a run that took him away across the yard. Harper returned his attention to Badger. The man was slumped in his saddle but was pulling a pocket-sized pistol into view. Badger fumbled with the weapon, almost dropped it, and made a feverish attempt to retain his hold on it.

'Throw it down,' Harper advised, 'or I'll kill you.'

Badger looked up, saw Harper's levelled gun, and bared his teeth in a grin of defiance. There was a spreading patch of blood on his shirt front. Harper wanted to take him alive, but Badger was of a mind to go down fighting. He used both hands to hold the gun, and grimaced as he struggled to bring it to bear. Harper waited as long as he dared, hoping the man would give up, but Badger eventually brought the gun into line and Harper fired a single shot. The bullet took Badger in the upper chest. He lost his hold on his gun and pitched sideways out of his saddle.

Harper stood with upraised gun, waiting to see whether Badger had had enough. The man crashed into the dust and remained motionless, his gun to one side. Harper heaved a sigh and looked around for Calder; he saw him riding hell for leather out of gunshot range. Harper went to Badger's side, bent over the man, and ascertained that he was dead. He picked up the discarded gun, a .41 two-shot derringer, and pushed it into a back pocket of his pants. As he straightened he could hear the echoes of the quick gun blasts fading away into the distance.

'What was that all about, Brad?' Bob Fuller was standing in the doorway of the house, having come through the interior from the back door. He was holding a gun, and looked ready to use it.

'Just a bit of law-dealing,' Harper replied, 'but I've got no idea what it was all about.'

He narrated the incident, and Fuller shook his head.

'Someone is jumping the gun about the Bar F,' Fuller observed. 'It hasn't been sold yet. Let's get on to town, Brad. I shall feel a lot easier with our prisoners behind bars.'

'I'll be looking up Calder as soon as I reach town,' Harper mused. 'I heard there was a new lumber business being set up, and it sure sounds like they are mixed up in this crooked deal. I want to stop off at the trading post on the way into Clear Spring. Kemp said he shot Joe Hilliard and Tom Caton in cold blood. I expect Hoose has made a run for it, but I'll pick him up if he hasn't.'

They went through the house to the back yard. Lily-Beth was standing to one side with Harper's Winchester in her hands, covering the prisoners although they were bound and tied to their saddles. Kemp was slumped in his saddle, barely conscious, and he groaned when the little cavalcade set out for town. Harper led with Kemp at his side, and Bob and Lily-Beth rode behind the other prisoners.

The afternoon was almost gone by the time Harper spotted the trading post in the distance. He reined into a draw and checked his pistol. His voice was flat and unemotional as he gave instructions to Fuller.

'Watch the prisoners, Bob, while I go for Hoose. Keep Lily-Beth here with you, and don't take any chances with Kemp. He looks like he's finished, but if you give him only half a chance he'll take advantage of it, and I want him alive. He knows a lot about what's been going on and we need proof to clean up on the bad men.'

'Don't worry about a thing,' Fuller replied. 'Go and do what you have to and these galoots will be here waiting when you get back.'

Harper rode on and circled the trading post to approach from an unexpected direction. The low building looked deserted, and there were no horses in the corral at the back. Harper dismounted behind the barn and trailed his reins. He went to the back door of the barn with his pistol in his hand and slipped inside the building, pausing to check the interior. Fargo was lying where he had fallen earlier. Harper moved on to the front door, remaining in concealment while he peered out to check the back yard. The silence was heavy, menacing, filled with hostility.

The back door of the trading post stood ajar. Harper eyed it speculatively for some moments. He was expecting a gun trap, for Dack Hoose was not a man to run away. He strode across the yard, avoiding the back entrance, then walked along the side of the store and paused at the left front corner to check the front yard of the single-storey building. Two motionless figures were lying in the dust in front of the door. Harper recognized them: Joe Hilliard and Tom Caton, the posse men. He heaved a sigh. Both men would still be alive if Kemp had been an honest deputy, and Harper blamed himself for not checking out his suspicions of Kemp when he should have done.

He reached a window beside the door and peered through the dusty glass. The interior of the trading post was gloomy, but Harper could see well enough to note that it was deserted. A creaking sound attracted his attention. He looked around quickly but saw nothing suspicious. The sound was repeated, and he glanced up at the roof just as a figure leapt down, feet first. He jerked up his pistol but a boot struck his arm and sent the weapon flying from his grasp. The man was upon him before he could react, and they both fell to the ground.

Hard knuckles cracked against Harper's left temple and his senses swirled at the impact. Harper grasped the man to smother the punches that came at him. He felt the outline of his pistol against his ribs as he rolled over it; he tried to snatch up the weapon as he moved clear, but a flurry of punches battered his head and he had to take evasive action. He slammed two hard rights into his attacker's stomach and heard the harsh sound of expelled breath in his ear. He lowered his head to avoid further punishment and threw his left fist at the man's jaw, his knuckles landing solidly on the target.

The man yelped and drew back. Harper slammed in several hard blows to the head before switching to the body. He felt the man wilt, and his punches stopped coming. The next instant pain flared in Harper's left side just above the waist, and he felt the point of a knife grating against his ribcage. The realization that he had been stabbed galvanized him into desperate action and he grabbed for the man's wrist, caught it, and twisted the arm until the knife fell to the ground. Harper kept twisting the limb, and suddenly the man was jerking away in an attempt to ease the intolerable pressure on his shoulder.

Harper got to his feet, maintaining the pressure on the man's arm. He had the advantage, for the man was twisting away to ease his limb. Harper leaned his weight on his left leg and lifted his right knee to the man's face. He repeated the action. The man was bending forward under the pressure applied to his arm and Harper's knee sent him over backwards. Harper released the arm as the man hit the ground and stepped in to kick at his head. The man relaxed instantly, and Harper turned and dived for his pistol.

With his gun in his hand, Harper faced his attacker. He recognized Bill Carney, who had ridden into the backyard earlier with the man called Skinny. Carney had shot Skinny accidentally when Harper attacked them. Harper nodded. So Hoose had apparently run out and left Carney to hold the fort. He stirred Carney with his boot. There was no reaction at first, and Harper waited until the man opened his eyes and looked around.

'OK,' Harper said. He pressed his left elbow into his side where the knife had caught him, looked down, saw blood spreading through his shirt. He ignored it for the moment. 'What happened here after I rode out?' he demanded.

Carney sat up. His face was swollen and there was blood trickling from his left ear. He rubbed his long jaw, opening his mouth like a fish out of water, then swallowed.

'Hoose said you'd be back,' he said sullenly. 'He lit out with a packhorse and left me to pick up the pieces. But I didn't do anything after you left. I was a prisoner with Hoose, and those two posse men were getting ready to take us into Clear Spring when a deputy sheriff rode in.' He paused and shook his head. 'I don't expect you to believe this, but the deputy shot those two posse men in cold blood. They were eating and he got behind them and gunned them down. He turned Hoose and me loose before he rode out.'

'I believe you,' Harper said. 'I've arrested Kemp on his own admission of shooting Caton and Hilliard. I've also got Frank Benton in irons and I've cleaned out the Benton ranch. I'll take you along with the rest of my prisoners and you can talk to the sheriff.'

Carney grimaced in shock and lapsed into silence. Harper moved back out of arm's length and examined the knife wound. The blade had glanced along his side, opening a gash about three inches long, but the ribs had deflected the weapon. The wound was painful but superficial. Harper took off his necker-chief, padded it against the gash, and held it in place with his left elbow pressed into his side.

'Where does Norton Calder come into this crooked business?' Harper asked.

Carney shook his head. 'I never heard of him,' he replied. 'I'm just a two-bit gun hand out to make a fast buck. Benton took me on a week ago and I just follow orders. I don't know what Benton's game is but he ain't a cattleman, and I ain't the type to ask questions. There's no future in this business if you're nosy.'

'I heard the name Stross mentioned,' Harper persisted. 'Who is he?'

'I got no idea.'

'So where is your horse? I'm in a hurry to hit town so let's get moving.'

Carney led the way round to the back yard. He staggered a couple of times but Harper sensed that he was hoping to steal an advantage and kept his distance. The man's horse was in a shed. He brought it out and led it to where Harper's buckskin was waiting.

'A word of warning,' Harper said as they rode out. 'Don't try to get smart. If you attempt to jump me I'll kill you. Head in that direction,' he pointed to the area where he had left Fuller and Lily-Beth with the prisoners, 'and don't even look round at me if you want to get to town in one piece.'

When they reached the spot where Bob Fuller had been left with the prisoners, Harper had a momentary pang of worry when he failed to spot the group, but Lily-Beth rode out of cover and approached him.

'Brad, you've been hurt!' the girl exclaimed. 'Are you OK?' She glared at Carney. 'Did you do that to him?'

'Never mind, Lily,' Harper cut in. 'Just keep an eye on him, and stay out of his reach. Shoot him if he tries to get away.'

'You can count on me,' Lily-Beth replied. 'We may have trouble coming, Brad. We hid in the gully because Bob spotted a couple of riders on our back trail heading this way. It looks like they are following our tracks. Bob is waiting for them to come into range.'

Harper drew his Winchester from its scabbard and handed it to the girl. 'Don't take any chances with him,' he warned.

He dismounted and entered the gully. His prisoners were still tied to their saddles but Kemp was down on the ground, semi-conscious. His condition seemed to have worsened since they left the Benton ranch. Bob Fuller was up on the rim of the gully, peering back the way they had come.

'Have we got trouble, Bob?' Harper demanded.

Fuller glanced down at Harper and grimaced. 'I can't say yet. A couple of riders are coming this way and they'll be in range in a few minutes. They are following our tracks so I expect they're looking for us. How do you want to handle this?'

'You stay where you are and cover me,' Harper replied. 'I'll challenge them when they draw nearer.'

He drew his pistol and checked the cylinder. His left side was giving him considerable pain but the bleeding had eased and he found it helped to keep his left elbow pressed against his bottom ribs. He moved back to the entrance to the gully, peered out along their back trail, and saw two riders approaching at a canter, watching the ground ahead of their mounts for tracks. Harper recognized Abe Hickman immediately. The AH rancher, short and heavily built, was solid in his saddle. He reined in quickly when

Harper stepped out of cover, and half-drew his holstered pistol before recognizing the deputy.

'You gave me a start, Brad,' Hickman greeted. 'I was on my way to town when I spotted tracks and decided to check them out. Jim Tolliver was raided last night. I saw the ruins of his house when I came by, and found Tolliver lying dead in a gully. That's why I'm feeling spooky. What the hell is going on around here? It was the Fuller place yesterday, and now Tolliver is gone. And what are you doing out here in the middle of nowhere? Have you seen more strangers around?'

'I sure have, and shot some of them,' Harper replied. 'I've got Frank Benton and a couple of his men tied to their saddles. And Joss Kemp showed up at the Benton place. I had to shoot him. He said he had killed Joe Hilliard and Tom Caton at Hoose's trading post. Do you know Benton, Abe? He's a nephew of Dan Benton, and took over Benton's spread a couple of weeks ago.'

'I heard he had showed up,' Hickman replied. 'What's he done?'

Harper explained and Hickman shook his head.

'So he's behind this trouble, huh?' the AH rancher mused.

'It looks that way.' Harper holstered his pistol. 'I'm gonna toss this business into the sheriff's lap. He'll soon get to the bottom of it. I don't think I've got all of the badmen. I heard a name mentioned of a man I haven't seen yet, and there is another who will be in town when I get there, so I'll be looking him up.'

'You're bleeding,' Hickman observed. 'Are you gonna be able to make it to town? I'll ride with you the rest of the way, just in case. Bill Redfern here is good with a gun, and we'll cover you in case someone else is planning to have a crack at you. If any more of those range stealers have come out into the open you're gonna be real busy.'

Harper nodded and led the way into the gully. Hickman paused when he saw

Kemp stretched out on the ground.

'So he's a badman, huh?' Hickman shook his head. 'I never cottoned to him, you know. There was always something about him that wasn't right. You should have killed him when you had the chance, Brad. There's nothing lower than a renegade lawman.'

'I want him alive,' Harper replied. 'He might be able to throw some light on what has been going on around here.'

Hickman looked hard at Lily-Beth. He turned to Bob Fuller and cursed mildly when he saw the extent of Fuller's injuries.

'Benton did this to you?' Hickman asked.

'He sure did,' Fuller replied. 'He planned to take the ranch from me — wanted it signed over to him.'

'That wouldn't have stood up in a court of law,' Hickman observed.

'They were going to kill me after I'd signed a quit note. They'd taken Lily-Beth, and would have killed her if

Brad hadn't got on to them.' Fuller's voice was ragged, and Harper, listening intently to what was being said, realized that his friend was under considerable strain from his recent experiences.

'Abe told me Jim Tolliver is lying dead out at his place and the ranch house has been burned down,' Harper said. He turned to the sullen Frank Benton. 'How many men are you running on this range?' he demanded. 'Did you think you could get away with murder and range stealing?'

Benton shook his head. 'You're talking to the wrong man,' he said. 'I don't know what you're talking about.'

Harper curbed his impatience. He had been thinking that catching Benton in the act of torturing Bob Fuller would have settled the trouble, but he realized he would have to visit the Tolliver spread to find out what had occurred there.

'Let's get moving,' he said sharply. 'If we don't push on we'll take all night to reach town.'

He went to Kemp's side and bent over the wounded ex-deputy. Kemp was conscious, and gazed at Harper without speaking. He made no comment when Harper pushed him into a saddle, and sat slumped as they set out for the distant town.

Harper was impatient to get the prisoners behind bars, and fretted inwardly as they continued. The trip seemed never-ending, and twice Kemp slid out of his saddle.

'You should have put him in a wagon,' Hickman observed the second time they halted to return Kemp to his saddle.

'He'll make it,' Harper replied as he thrust Kemp back into leather.

The sun set in a blaze of red-gold fire and shadows crawled across the range. The heat of the day eased. Harper tried to relax. He was satisfied with the way his efforts had turned out, but had a nagging feeling in the back of his mind when he thought of Jim Tolliver. He remained beside Kemp, but kept a close watch on his other prisoners. Bob Fuller was riding stoically at the rear with Lily-Beth by his side. Hickman sided Fuller, and chatted non-stop with the young cattleman.

They stopped several times on the long trip. Full darkness settled around them and the hours passed. When they eventually saw the lights of Clear Spring ahead Harper guessed the time was around midnight, and he heaved a sigh of relief when he reined up in front of the sheriff's office.

Hickman hurried into the office to talk to Mort Bland. The sheriff came out to the sidewalk as Harper dragged Kemp from his saddle. Kemp's knees buckled and he sagged into the dust. Harper lifted him and half-carried him into the office while giving the sheriff an account of what had occurred during the long day. Bland listened in a stony silence, shaking his head from time to time. He uttered a low groan when heard that Joe Hilliard and Tom Caton were dead, and when he checked

Bob Fuller to assess his injuries he gave vent to his anger.

'Let's get these galoots behind bars,' he said. 'Brad, fetch Doc Carter, and when he's treated the injured we'll get statements. Then you'd better head out to the Tolliver place and look around.'

'There's a man in town I want to see before I do anything else,' Harper said, 'but I guess he can wait until morning. His name is Norton Calder, and he's running the new sawmill in town. I reckon he's got some explaining to do.'

The prisoners were locked in the cells. Lily-Beth stifled a yawn and Harper, watching her, tried to assess the degree of her exhaustion. He was bone-weary and nearing the end of his strength, for it had been an exhausting twenty-four hours.

'What are we going to do?' Lily-Beth asked Fuller.

'I guess we'll spend the night in here,' Bob replied. 'I'm not taking any chances after this. We don't know who else is mixed up in this crooked business, and we'd be foolish to go back to the ranch and run into more trouble. You said the house was burned last night, and I reckon you won't fancy sleeping in the barn anyway. We'd better stay in town until we are certain the law has sorted out our problems.'

Harper tucked his left elbow against his ribs. Darting pangs of agony were giving him great discomfort.

'I'll fetch Doc Carter,' he said. 'It looks like most of us need medical treatment, and I'm gonna have to change my clothes.'

He left the office and paused outside in the shadows to lean against the front wall of the office to relax for a moment. He closed his eyes, fighting against the insidious spread of weakness trying to envelop him. But he was aware that nothing would help but a good rest. He pushed himself wearily into motion and continued along the street to the doctor's house.

Doc Carter was easily awakened, and opened his door surprisingly quickly.

'Brad, what in tarnation happened to you?' Carter demanded. 'Have you been fighting a wildcat? Come on in and I'll take a look at you.'

'There's plenty of work for you at the jail,' Harper countered. 'I've brought in the men responsible for the trouble at Bob Fuller's place, and there was some shooting — '

'Give me the facts while I'm treating you,' Carter interrupted. 'Say, you've lost a lot of blood, and you're not looking too fierce.'

Harper nodded, and sat with his eyes closed while Carter treated him. He gave an account of what had occurred, and was feeling easier by the time the doctor had finished his ministrations. He pushed himself wearily to his feet and clutched at the doctor when the room appeared to tilt and swing.

'Steady,' Carter warned. 'What you need now is a good night's sleep. You'll feel much better in the morning, so go home to bed now and come and see me tomorrow.'

'I'm riding out again as soon as I've changed my shirt,' Harper explained.

'I don't think you'll get very far,' Carter opined. 'If you don't rest now you won't be fit for anything in the morning. But I know it is no use advising you, Brad. I guess you'll do what you have to. Come on, I'd better get to the jail and do what I can there.'

They walked along the street to the law office. Hickman and his rider, Redfern, were leading the horses away to the livery barn. Inside the office, Bob Fuller was making a statement of his experiences at the hands of Frank Benton. Lily-Beth was seated beside her brother, her expression revealing the extent of her horror as she listened to his stark account. Before Harper could say anything Doc Carter informed the sheriff that his only deputy was not fit for duty. Bland looked intently at Harper and then nodded.

'I guess you're right, Doc. I reckon he's had a bad twenty-four hours. OK, Brad, you stick around town and get statements from all concerned. I've had it easy around here so I'll ride out to the Tolliver place, and I'll take a couple of posse men along. Hickman is staying in the hotel tonight. He's told Bill Redfern to stick around here to help out, and said he'd send a couple of his men into town tomorrow to give us a hand with law dealing. I reckon I'll take advantage of his offer until I can appoint a new deputy. The trouble is, there won't be many volunteers for the job now we got trouble on our hands.'

Harper nodded, feeling disinclined to argue with the sheriff.

'I'd better get moving.' Bland got to his feet. 'I want to be at Tolliver's by sunup. You take it easy around here, Brad. Rest up as much as you can, and call in a couple of the regular posse men to help out. We've got to get the upper hand in this business.' He paused, eyed Harper speculatively, then asked: 'Are you sure you can handle this?'

Harper nodded, and walked to the

door with the sheriff.

'OK, I'll be back some time tomorrow,' Bland said, and departed.

Harper went to the desk and sat down to work on Bob Fuller's statement, but Doc Carter intervened.

'I'll check Bob over now,' he said firmly. 'Your statements can wait, Brad.'

Harper nodded. He looked at Lily-Beth, saw her stifle a yawn, and decided to take a firm line with her. She was looking strained, and he could only guess at the stress she was experiencing after the tensions of the previous twenty-four hours.

'Lily, why don't you get some rest in the sheriff's quarters? He won't be using his bed tonight, and you look kind of all in. If you can sleep for a few hours you'll feel a whole lot better in the morning.'

To his surprise Lily-Beth nodded.

'I am at the end of my rope,' she agreed. 'Can we get some coffee at this time of the night?'

'There's a kitchen out back. Why

don't you make coffee for all of us?'

She nodded, and Harper led her through the cell block to the sheriff's private quarters. Lily-Beth looked around the small kitchen. Harper put a match to the stove, which was already laid, and the girl began the routine of coffee-making.

Harper opened a door leading off from the kitchen to reveal a small bedroom. 'You can bunk down in here, Lily, and the sooner you put your head down the better. I'd rather you stayed here tonight where I can keep an eye on you, just in case. This business isn't over yet, not by a long rope, and you won't be safe until I've flushed out all the badmen.'

Lily-Beth nodded tiredly. Harper went back into the office. Doc Carter was bandaging the worst of Fuller's injuries.

'They sure got nasty with you, Bob,' Carter commented. 'It's a good thing you held out against them or we'd be arranging your funeral now.'

'I was aware that the moment I signed my name on the dotted line I'd be as good as dead,' Fuller replied. 'Have you got some place I can get my head down, Brad? I'm feeling plumb tuckered out right now.'

'A cell is the best I can do,' Harper replied. 'You and Lily should stay here tonight. I'd like to be able to keep an eye on you.'

'And I'm gonna back you all the way,' Fuller replied.

The street door opened and Bill Redfern appeared.

'Hickman told me to stand by here tonight and help out,' Redfern said. 'I just put our horses in the livery barn, and while I was there I got a feeling I was being watched from cover. I didn't see anyone, but I reckon if I'd been you, Harper, something might have happened.'

Harper became intent. 'I'll go along there and check it out,' he said, drawing his pistol and checking its loads.

'You can't just walk in there,' Redfern

said. 'It felt like I'd walked into a gun trap. I could feel hairs lifting on the back of my neck, and yet I didn't see a thing. But I'd stake my life on someone being in that barn waiting for a particular person to show up. I've been around some, Harper, and I've learned to trust my feelings.'

'Thanks for the tip, but I have to do my job,' Harper replied firmly. 'I'm impatient to put an end to this business. If you'll stick around here and watch the jail I'll be able to go with an easy mind.'

'Anything you say.' Redfern nodded. 'It would be unwise to leave your prisoners unguarded right now. The way I figure it, someone might be waiting for you to leave the jail so they can bust your prisoners loose, and you don't want to lose anyone after the trouble you've had picking them up.'

Harper nodded and holstered his pistol. 'Keep this street door locked at all times,' he instructed, 'and don't let anyone in here you don't know.'

He departed then, and stood on the sidewalk to hear Redfern bolt the door. The main street was filled with dense shadows. Only an oil lamp burned here and there in windows along its length. The silence was heavy, fraught with hostility. Harper shrugged his shoulders. He had a job to do, and the sooner he got on with it the better.

His boots thudded on the boards of the sidewalk so he stepped into the dust of the street. His alertness was at its peak, and he kept his right hand close to the butt of his pistol, ready to flow into action at the first sign of trouble. He saw a dim light inside the saloon, and guessed a late poker game was in progress in one of the back rooms. He noted that the door beyond the batwings was not closed and paused to check it.

At that moment a man thrust his way out of the saloon, setting the batwings swinging violently. Harper was startled and drew his gun. The man paused on the boardwalk, hunching forward to get

131

a closer look at Harper, who was shrouded in shadow.

'Is that you, Brad?' the man demanded, Harper recognized the voice as that of Sim Archer, who owned the general store. 'Say you're getting a mite nervous, ain't you? Why are you prowling around at this time of the night with your gun out? Are you looking for trouble?'

'I don't have to look for trouble, Sim,' Harper replied. 'It knows where to find me.'

He went on until he reached the end of the sidewalk and stood in the shadows looking at the livery barn, steeling himself, for he had to go in there and check it out, aware that a trap might have been laid for him.

6

Harper fought against encroaching tiredness and forced his mind to full alertness. He considered the situation, aware that he had a choice of action; he could enter the stable openly and be ready to shoot it out with whoever was holed up inside, or he could sneak in by the back door and play them at their own game — stalk them and steal the initiative. He decided instantly to brace whoever was in the barn by entering brazenly. If someone was waiting, especially for him, then that someone would have to identify his intended victim before resorting to gunplay.

He held his gun cocked and ready for action as he strode across the open space to the big front door of the barn. This was how it should be, he told himself. He was capable of handling this situation without getting himself killed, and was not afraid of bad men who skulked through the shadows and shot from cover. He reached a front corner of the barn and paused to listen, heard nothing unnatural, and then tip-toed along the front wall to the big open door. He froze all movement when he heard a horse stamp inside the barn and restrained his breathing to listen intently. When no further sound emanated from the interior he got down and eased forward close to the ground until he was able to enter the barn and slither to the right of the doorway.

The silence was intense. He tried to pierce the surrounding blackness but was unable to make out any details inside the barn. He could feel sweat trickling down the hollow of his chest, and battled to control his nerves, needing all of his ability at its best if he would overcome this situation; aware that all he had to do was wait for impatience to come to his aid. If a gun trap had been set up in the barn the men who were waiting would surely get cramped and decide eventually to withdraw.

He eased himself into a sitting position with his back against the inside of the front wall about ten feet to the right of the big doorway, holding his gun ready. He made fresh demands on his patience — fought his tiredness when it threatened to betray him. As time passed he felt his eyelids grow heavy and begin to close, but he held on, determined to wait until sunup if he had to. He needed a break in this business and as far as he could see he had nothing to lose, except his life if he called the wrong shots.

His mind was active while he waited. He reconsidered everything which had occurred since he rode out of town the day before and could not fault his own actions. He had done everything right; he felt that he was ahead in this grim game, and all he had to do now was retain the initiative.

He began to drowse without realizing it, and he jerked up, startled, when a horse whickered softly in the darkness. He looked around for some moments, trying to regain his concentration, and was wondering just how long he had been unaware of his surroundings when a voice called in an undertone from somewhere in the surrounding shadows.

'Hey, Shreeve, ain't it about time we called this off? That damn deputy won't be coming now. Someone else brought those horses in, and I'm betting one of them was the deputy's mount. We're wasting our time here. We should be with the others, getting ready to hit the jail and bust Benton loose. I could sure do with a drink so let's cut the pussyfooting and get out of here.'

'Jeez, Buster, why don't you shout so the whole town can hear you? Just button your lip. We got our orders and all we have to do is obey them. What they are gonna do at the jail ain't our business, so just stay still and wait it out.'

Harper was now fully alert. It was

impossible to pinpoint the exact position of the two men and he waited, his breathing restrained and every nerve in his body ready to precipitate action. He was shocked by the information that an attempt was to be made to break into the jail, and wished he could have been in two places at once. His mind began insisting that he do something to break the deadlock.

He plucked a .45 cartridge from a loop in his belt and tossed it into the darkness, ready to shoot if it brought a reaction from the two men. The cartridge struck a metal object with a sharp sound which was amplified in the heavy silence, and the interior of the barn blazed instantly with gunflame and thunder. One of the men emptied a pistol wildly into the surrounding shadows and slugs flew in all directions. Harper aimed for the gun flashes and squeezed his trigger. His pistol kicked against the heel of his hand and added flashing noise to the disturbance. He squirmed to his right a couple of yards, eyes narrowed to observe the action, and two slugs thudded into the woodwork at his back within a couple of inches of his head.

Harper fired again, pinpointing the muzzle flame piercing the shadows. He heard a cry of agony amidst the thunder of the shot and waited with his gun poised, but the echoes faded away into silence and all he could hear were the restless sounds of the horses alarmed by the shooting. He fancied that he had hit both men but he remained in cover, waiting with growing impatience.

'Hello, the barn,' a voice called suddenly from outside the big front door. 'Who is in there? You better come on out with your hands up. We've got the place surrounded and you have two minutes to show yourself or we'll come in and get you.'

Harper grinned as he recognized the voice of Pete Halfnight, one of the town carpenters. Halfnight was a great believer in law and order, a stalwart of the regular town posse that Mort Bland had organized. He never missed a ride for the law, and breathed fire and brimstone whenever action became imminent.

'Pete,' Harper called. 'This is Brad Harper. I braced a couple of men in here and I think I've nailed them, but they could be lying doggo. Put a lantern on a pole and stick it in through the doorway and I'll take it from there.'

'OK, Brad. Give me a couple of minutes.'

Harper waited tensely, his gun ready. He heard nothing from the two men. Were they dead or playing possum? He waited out the tense moments. The surrounding silence was intense. But suddenly a faint gleam of yellow light pierced the shadows and he heard footsteps approaching the barn.

'Are you ready for the light, Brad?' Halfnight called.

'Sure.' Harper lifted his gun.

A lantern tied to a pole was thrust into the doorway about four feet above the ground and yellow light chased out the darkness. Harper peered around, and saw two men stretched out only feet apart and apparently dead. Their guns were lying on the ground. Harper got to his feet, covering both figures, and went forward to check them. One was dead, shot through the heart, and the other was unconscious with blood staining his shirtfront.

'OK, Pete,' Harper called. Halfnight came into the barn and brought the lantern across to highlight the two men.

Harper looked at the stiffening faces and saw two strangers. He glanced at the intent Halfnight, who was gazing stolidly at the men.

'I've never seen them before, Pete,' Harper observed.

'I have.' Halfnight nodded. 'They're a couple of the crew that is setting up the new sawmill in town. I had a visit yesterday from a man called Norton Calder who is managing the business. He showed me their set-up, and gave me a good deal to buy my lumber from them when they are up and running. I remember seeing these two men in the mill, making trestles and the like, and I heard the saws working this afternoon, so they aren't wasting any time. But what were they doing setting up a gun trap?'

'That's what I mean to find out,' Harper said softly. 'Fetch Doc Carter, Pete, and stick around until I get back. There could be trouble waiting for me at the law office.'

'Is it anything I should get involved in?' Halfnight demanded.

'No. Just stick around here until Doc Carter has been in. I'd better get moving.'

Harper reloaded his pistol and set off back along the street towards the law office. He needed to arrest Norton Calder, but was worried about the security of the jail. The street was quiet and, as he walked along its centre where the shadows were densest, he saw several figures, attracted by the shooting, in the shadows on the sidewalk heading towards the livery barn. He made for the alley across the street from the law office, where he stood looking around, listening intently. Shreeve and Buster had mentioned an attempt to break out the prisoners, and he intended being on hand to thwart it.

A lantern was alight in the law office and he could see the interior through the front window. There was no movement inside, and when he was satisfied that no one was watching the jail he crossed the street and peered through the window. Redfern was seated at the desk reading an old newspaper, and Harper turned away, reluctant to disturb the peace. He crossed the street again to check out the alley and the surrounding area for intruders.

An hour passed before Harper was satisfied that no unlawful action was being planned against the jail. He made a circuit of the street and walked through the alleys on either side. He saw Doc Carter enter the barn, leave again almost immediately, and assumed that the second man inside had died. His thoughts were bleak as he moved silently through the shadows back to the alley across the street from the jail and stepped into its cover to continue watching for trouble. He closed his eyes and rubbed them tiredly, and at that moment a slight noise at his back jerked him back to full alertness.

Harper dropped his hand to his gun butt as he swung around, but before he could draw the weapon a hand came out of the inky darkness and grabbed his wrist to prevent his draw. He reacted swiftly, swinging his left hand, the knuckles bunched into a fist, but before he could connect with his assailant a heavy object slammed against his skull and oblivion over-whelmed him. He fell heavily to the ground as if dropping into a grave on boot hill. A flaring light seared through his brain, and then sight and sound faded and total blackout claimed him.

He had no idea how long he was unconscious, and his first intimation of returning to his senses was a throbbing pain inside his skull beating with an insistence which had him groaning, his eyes tightly closed. Nausea was churning in his stomach. He was lying on his back and made an effort to get on to his left side. He lifted a hand to his head and pressed his fingers against the spot where he had been struck in a vain attempt to ease the agony which gripped him. He managed to get into a sitting position with his back pressed against the wall of the alley and his chin on his chest.

Full alertness returned slowly, and eventually he was able to lift his head, open his eyes, and look around into the darkness. The light emanating from the law office caught his gaze and he stared fixedly at it, trying to make the effort to get to his feet. He placed his hands on the ground to lever himself up and discovered his pistol by his side. He grasped the weapon, pushed himself to his knees, and eventually made it to his feet.

He staggered across the street, his gaze fixed on the light in the office. He suspected that something was wrong when he reached out to open the office door and discovered that it was not closed. He paused when the door swung open to his touch, and the first thing he noticed inside was that Redfern was no longer seated at the desk.

Harper entered the office with his gun levelled. He crossed to the door leading into the cells, which was unlocked, and thrust it open. A lantern was alight inside the cell block and he looked around, horrified to find his prisoners gone. The back door was ajar. He shook his head and groaned softly at the surge of pain which darted through it. Then he saw a movement in one of the cells. He went to the door to find Bob Fuller lying trussed on the bunk with a gag in his mouth and a bruise on his forehead.

Harper entered the cell and untied Fuller, who sat up and held his head.

'What happened, Bob?' Harper demanded.

'Two men came in here pushing Redfern ahead of them. Redfern had his hands up. They turned Benton and the others loose and left by the back door, taking Redfern with them. Before they left, Benton came in here waving a gun. He told me they didn't need me any more — the deal had changed. Then Benton hit me with his gun barrel, and when I woke up I was tied hand and foot.'

'And what happened to Lily-Beth?' Harper demanded.

Fuller shook his head. Harper crossed to the door leading to the sheriff's private quarters, thrust it open, then halted in mid-stride, for Lily-Beth was sleeping peacefully on the sheriff's bunk. He studied her for some moments before closing the door.

'Is she OK?' Fuller demanded.

'Sleeping like a babe,' Harper replied. 'I'll let her sleep.'

'I've been thinking while lying here like a trussed chicken,' Fuller mused.

He was sitting on the edge of the bunk in the cell and massaging his forehead. 'How did those two men get into the office? I heard you tell Redfern not to admit anyone he didn't know.'

'So obviously he knew them,' Harper observed. 'You said Redfern came in here with his hands up. Did he have his pistol in its holster or had he been disarmed?'

'I don't know. The two men pushed him around, and one of them held a gun on him. I didn't notice anything else.'

'And those two men,' Harper asked. 'Did you know them or were they strangers?'

Fuller shook his head. 'I'd never seen them before, Brad. There are so many strangers around here now. But I reckon I would know them again if I ever set eyes on them.'

Harper nodded. 'That's worth remembering.' He pressed a hand against his head for a moment. 'I guess there's nothing I can do about this situation until morning,' he decided. 'Try and get some sleep, Bob. I'll make the place secure and we'll wait for sunup.'

'I doubt I shall be able to sleep,' Fuller replied. 'My head is pounding and I don't know what is going on any more. Benton said they didn't need me now. Does that mean they've given up trying to steal my ranch?'

'They don't have much chance of succeeding now their crooked plan is out in the open,' Harper observed. 'But don't worry about it right now. I'll get some answers tomorrow. You're not the only one with a sore head, Bob, so let's settle down and get some rest, huh? I reckon I've done enough for today.'

Fuller nodded and stretched out on the bunk. Harper went to the back door and locked it. The bunch of jail keys was hanging from the key in the back door. He removed all the keys and went through to the front office. He closed the front door and locked it, then went to the desk and sank into the chair behind it; he placed his elbows on the desk and lowered his aching head into his hands.

He was bone-weary but did not think he would be able to sleep because of the insistent pounding inside his skull and the flood of thoughts whirling around in his brain. He closed his eyes wearily. The next thing he was aware of was lifting his head and peering at sunlight creeping in through the front window. He winced as his senses whirled when he sprang to his feet, and had to lean his hands on the desk and close his eyes until the throbbing eased.

A noise at the door leading into the cells had him whirling round. He saw Fuller entering the office. The sight of Fuller's badly bruised face made Harper overlook his own aches and pains and he straightened.

'How are you feeling this morning, Bob?' Harper enquired.

'Better than I was feeling this time yesterday. But I can't put two and two together about this business, Brad. Have you got any idea what is going on?'

'I think I have a grip on its tail, and there are a couple of men I need to see today.'

'Do you think Benton was giving me the truth when he said he was no longer interested in my spread?'

'They had no choice but to pull out when I caught them in the act. I expect their whole deal will fall through now. Give Lily-Beth a call and we'll get some breakfast. Then I have work to do. But I'd better take a look out back and see which way Benton rode off last night.'

Fuller accompanied Harper through the cell block and they went out to the back lot. The hoofprints of several horses showed clearly in the dust and Harper checked them closely.

'It looks like Benton took out fast,' Harper observed. 'The sheriff should be back some time today, and when he shows up I'll track Benton down.'

'I'd like to ride with you,' Fuller said harshly.

'I reckon you should stick around town for a day or two, just in case

Benton was bluffing about giving up on you. There's Lily-Beth to consider. She had a bad time of it yesterday and you've got to shield her from more of the same.'

'I guess you're right.' Fuller nodded. 'But I sure would like to get the drop on Benton and give him some of his own medicine.'

They went back into the law office. Harper heard someone banging on the street door. He jerked it open to find Abe Hickman standing on the sidewalk. The AH rancher's horse was hitched to a nearby rail.

'Where is Redfern?' Hickman demanded. 'It's time we were heading back to the ranch.'

Harper explained the events of the night and Hickman's expression changed.

'The hell you say!' he exclaimed. 'And they took Redfern with them when they left? Why would they want to drag him along?'

'That's something I mean to find out,' Harper said. 'How long has

Redfern been working for you, Abe?'

'Three years, and I trust him with my life.' Hickman frowned. 'Are you thinking he had something to do with your prisoners escaping?'

'I don't know anything for certain right now, but I will get to the bottom of it before I'm through,' Harper replied.

'If Redfern shows up around here then tell him to return to the ranch.' Hickman turned away and went to his horse. He swung into the saddle and then looked down at Harper. 'If you need any help to sort out this trouble then let me know and I'll bring my outfit into town to back you,' he said.

'Thanks for the offer.' Harper watched with speculation in his eyes as Hickman lifted a hand in farewell, set spurs to his mount, and rode off in a cloud of dust.

Lily-Beth was in the office when Harper turned around. The girl was looking as if she had not slept at all during the night. Her face was pale and drawn, and she seemed exhausted.

'I hope you're feeling better than you look,' Harper observed. Lily-Beth smiled.

'I'm getting over my shock now,' she replied. 'But Bob has just told me about the escape last night. And I never heard a thing. Do you think Benton has really given up?'

'That's what he told Bob, and I can think of no reason to doubt him, but I wouldn't trust him an inch. I think you and Bob should stick around town at least until the sheriff gets back.'

'That's what I told Bob. I need more time to get over what happened yesterday.'

'Let's get some breakfast, and then I'll start my job,' Harper replied.

Harper called Fuller out of the office and locked the door. They walked along the street to the diner, which was busy, but they found a vacant table. Harper discovered he was ravenous and ate a large breakfast. But impatience was nagging in his mind and he left the diner as soon as he could get away from Bob and Lily-Beth. He paused on the sidewalk outside the diner to check his pistol, and glanced over his shoulder when Fuller spoke to him.

'I want to go along with you, Brad,' Fuller said.

Harper knew by the tone in Fuller's voice that it would be useless arguing so he nodded.

'Just don't get under my feet if I get lucky and cotton on to someone,' he replied.

'So where do we start looking for bad men?' Fuller spoke in a determined tone. He gripped the butt of a pistol protruding from his waistband which he had picked up in the law office.

Harper could hear the distant sound of a circular saw ripping through lumber, and turned in the direction from which it came, aware that it was time he braced Norton Calder.

'Just stay in the background, Bob,' he ordered.

Fuller nodded. They walked to the outskirts of the town to a large barn and a couple of big sheds which were

154

standing on a back lot. The place had been used by a freighting company in the past, but the outfit had pulled out when the railroad reached Dodge City. Now there was a huge pile of lumber in front of the big open door of the barn, and the screeching whine of a steam-driven saw sounded continually.

Harper paused in the doorway of the barn and looked inside. A small steam engine was supplying power to drive a big saw, and dust was drifting as four men toiled at their work. There was no sign of Norton Calder, and Harper looked around for an office. A big man wearing a brown dustcoat came forward from the back of the barn and accosted Harper. He was large-boned, fleshy, and had a pugnacious jaw which jutted forward even more as he eyed Harper's law star and then glanced at the gun holstered on Harper's hip.

'If you've come about Shreeve and Buster then you're out of luck,' the man said harshly. 'Calder is away on a trip and won't be back for several days.'

'Why would I want to see Calder about a couple of men who tried to kill me last night?' Harper countered. 'Was he their keeper?' He paused for a reply but the man merely shook his head. 'So what's your name?' Harper continued.

'I'm Ernie Mitchell, the foreman here. What can I do for you?'

'You can do nothing for me unless you know why two of your men tried to kill me last night.'

'I don't know a thing about that. I ain't their keeper either.' Mitchell grinned.

Harper's left hand shot out and grasped the front of Mitchell's coat. He pulled the big man forward and thrust upwards until Mitchell was standing on his toes.

'Do you think it is funny that two men tried to kill me and are dead?' he demanded.

'Hell no, I don't!' Mitchell lifted a hand to Harper's left wrist and tried to break the hold on his coat. He failed. He became passive and gazed into

Harper's determined face. 'You killed Shreeve and Buster and that leaves me two men short this morning,' he complained. 'I have a schedule to maintain and I'm way behind at the moment.'

'I don't like your manner, Mitchell.' Harper released his grip on the man's coat. 'You'd better practise being helpful or you'll find more trouble than you can handle when I come again. Now turn off that saw so I can hear myself speak. I want to talk to those three men.'

'I can't stop them working.' Mitchell straightened his coat. 'If you want to talk to them then come back when they've finished working for the day.'

'Keep talking like that and you'll spend the rest of the day behind bars,' Harper said sharply. 'Hop to it, Mitchell, or you'll be sorry you ever set foot in this town.'

Mitchell looked into Harper's impassive gaze and realized he had gone as far as he could. He nodded and made a motion with his right hand, palm down. One of the three men working on the saw turned and switched it off. Harper pushed Mitchell in the back and they walked across to the work site. The three workers stood motionless, watching Harper intently; he noted that all three were wearing gun belts. Fuller tagged along behind, and halted a couple of paces to Harper's right when they reached the trio.

'The deputy wants a few words with you,' Mitchell said loudly. 'And talk easy because he's on the warpath.'

'There's no need for talk, Brad,' Bob Fuller said sharply, pulling a pistol from his waistband. 'That guy on the right was one of the two men who came into the jail in the night and busted Benton and the others loose.'

Harper reached for his pistol at Fuller's words. Mitchell swung to grab hold of Harper's wrist. Out of the corner of his eye Harper saw the other three lumbermen reaching for their holstered guns. Then all hell broke loose.

7

Harper's mind was filled with protest as he drew his pistol, for he needed prisoners who could talk. He evaded Mitchell's clutching hand and grabbed the man's shoulder to thrust him off balance, at the same time lifting his gun into action. The three lumbermen were intent on resistance, and Fuller's gun exploded raucously, his slug sending one of the lumbermen spinning around to fall across a pile of freshly sawn planks. Harper cocked his gun and aimed for the right shoulder of a second man. His gun hammered; the man dropped his gun and fell face down on the ground. Gun echoes were heavy inside the barn and reverberated in the distance.

Mitchell was apparently unarmed. He overbalanced when Harper pushed him, then fell to his knees, where he remained unmoving, his hands in plain view. The third lumberman changed his mind about drawing his pistol when the weapon was only halfway clear of his holster. He thrust it deep into leather and lifted his hands shoulder high.

Fuller ran forward and disarmed the man. Harper covered Mitchell, who had lifted his right hand to a pocket of his long dustcoat.

'If you've got a gun in that pocket then be mighty careful how you pull it,' Harper advised.

Mitchell withdrew his hand from the pocket. He was clutching a short-barrelled pistol. He threw down as if it had suddenly become red-hot.

'On your feet,' Harper rapped, and Mitchell arose.

'The guy I shot is dead,' Fuller called excitedly. He bent over the man Harper had shot. 'This one is still breathing. It looks like you got yourself some more prisoners, Brad.'

'Let's get them to the jail,' Harper replied. 'I wanted their boss, Norton

Calder, because he threw down on me yesterday at Benton's place, but I'll pick him up when he comes back to town.' He waved his pistol at Mitchell. 'You and the other guy pick up the wounded man and head for the jail. Then we'll get down to business. I want to know why a dozen men came into this town to operate a sawmill and then got mixed up in a land-steal.'

Mitchell did not reply. The wounded man was picked up and carried out of the barn. As they made their way to the main street several townsmen appeared, some carrying guns, and came towards them. Harper recognized them as posse men, and saw Pete Halfnight carrying a double-barrelled shotgun with which he covered the prisoners.

'What happened, Brad?' Halfnight demanded. 'Those are the sawyers from the new mill. What was the shooting about?'

'Tag along, keep your ears open, and you'll learn the facts,' Harper replied. 'I'm gonna need a couple of the posse men to guard the jail until the sheriff gets back from Jim Tolliver's place.'

'I'll handle it,' Halfnight said eagerly. 'I ain't got a job to do this morning, and Bill Moore can side me. He's off work for a couple of days.'

Lily-Beth was standing in the doorway of the hotel talking to Doc Carter. They tagged along behind the party. Doc Carter questioned Bob Fuller incessantly as the group entered the law office. Harper called for silence because everyone was talking at once. He ordered Halfnight to lock the prisoners in cells and mount guard over them. Silence returned when the doctor followed the prisoners to check them over. Harper heaved a sigh. He was beginning to feel that the whole situation was descending into chaos.

The door opened and Sim Archer, the storekeeper, stuck his head round it.

'Have you got a minute, Brad?' he demanded.

'Can it wait?' Harper grimaced. 'I'm up to my neck in it right now, Sim.'

'I think you should stop what you're doing and take a look in my barn back of the store,' Archer replied. 'I went to get a couple of crates of stock and found the lock busted. When I looked inside I saw Bill Redfern sprawled on the floor, knifed in the chest.'

'Redfern!' Harper repeated. 'Bob, stand by here until I get back, huh?'

Fuller nodded and Harper departed with Archer.

'I don't know what this town is coming to,' Archer declared as they made their way to the back lots. 'I've noticed that the trouble started when that saw mill began operating. The men working there all carry guns, and that ain't normal, Brad. Working men don't need to be armed around town, and until now we've never had any trouble around here.'

'We've sure got more than our fair share of it now,' Harper responded. 'But we are getting on top of it, Sim.'

A couple of men were standing in the open doorway of the storekeeper's barn. They began talking excitedly but Harper pushed them aside and entered the barn, to find Bill Redfern stretched out on the floor, his shirt stained with blood.

'I haven't touched him or anything,' Archer said. 'I could see he was dead so I came for you.'

'You did right,' Harper replied.

'I'm wondering what he's doing in here,' Archer mused. 'Who would want to kill him?'

'I sure wish I knew the answer to that question.' Harper shook his head. 'Put a new lock on the door and shut the barn tight until I can get back here.'

'Can I take out the stock I need?' Archer demanded.

'I'll wait until you've done so and then take the key with me. Make it quick, Sim, I'm up to my ears in it this morning.'

Harper waited patiently. Archer removed his stock and then returned with a new lock. The door was secured and Harper took the key.

'Keep quiet about this, Sim,' Harper advised, and made his way back to the law office.

Bob Fuller's expression mirrored the uncertainty Harper was feeling when he learned of Redfern's death. He shook his head and looked at Harper with questions in his eyes.

'Don't look to me for answers, Bob,' Harper said. 'I'm out of my depth in this business and it seems to be getting more and more difficult with every killing. I sure wish the sheriff was back here to take over.'

'You haven't done too badly so far,' Fuller protested. 'I'll bet Mort Bland couldn't have done as much had he been here. All you've got to do now is question your prisoners and get at the truth. It is obvious that Benton is guilty of a number of crimes, mainly against Lily-Beth and me, and that those men at the sawmill are mixed up in it somehow.'

'I got it figured out that far,' Harper replied, 'but I need more than that to take before the judge.'

'Get the truth out of the prisoners,' Fuller insisted. 'After what was done to me I'd take great pleasure in making them talk.'

Harper shook his head. He went to the door between the office and the cells and looked in, to see Doc Carter treating the wounded man. Halfnight was watching intently, his shotgun in his hands.

'Bring Mitchell out here, Pete,' Harper said, and Halfnight obeyed.

Mitchell was brought into the office and made to sit in a chair before the desk. Halfnight stood behind the sawyer. Harper could tell by Mitchell's expression that the man would admit nothing, but he decided to go through the motions of interrogation.

'How come you're mixed up in this trouble, Mitchell?' he asked.

'I'm not mixed up in anything,' Mitchell replied easily. 'I was only doing what I get paid for. I was told I could expect trouble from some of the local men because they are against a sawmill operating in this county, and I was merely doing my job. If that is against the law then I'm guilty.'

Harper grinned. 'I've never heard such a poor reason to explain gunplay,' he observed. 'You're gonna have to do much better than that. You and your lumbermen were armed and didn't hesitate to pull your guns when I showed up at the mill. I need a statement from you, and the sooner you open up about what has been happening around here the better.'

'All I know is what I am doing at the mill,' Mitchell said stolidly. 'You'll have to talk to Calder when he gets back. Maybe he can help you.'

Harper suppressed a sigh and glanced at the attentive Halfnight. 'OK, Pete, put him back in his cell. I'm wasting my time, and he'll keep until the sheriff gets back.'

'I'd get the truth out of him,' Fuller said. 'Let me spend ten minutes in that cell with him.'

Harper shook his head. 'Not now, Bob. There are other things to handle.'

'Yeah, like finding Redfern's killer, huh?' Fuller grimaced. 'I've been thinking about that. Why did he open the office door to those two men who busted the prisoners loose? And did they kill him after they got away from here?'

'There are a lot of questions that need answers,' Harper replied. 'One that bothers me is who sent the two men to turn the prisoners loose?'

Fuller's expression hardened. 'I never thought of that! And at the same time two other men were laying a gun trap for you in the livery barn. Just how many men are working for this bunch that's causing the trouble, and who is bossing the outfit?'

'I might get the answers to those questions when I pick up Norton Calder.' Harper glanced out of the window when he heard the sound of hoofs in the street. He saw Mort Bland riding in and relief swept through him. 'It's the sheriff,' he said, and hastened to the door, hoping that with the old lawman's help he could make some progress with his investigation.

Sheriff Bland stepped down from his saddle and stretched as he glanced around the street. He was tired, and his face showed the rigours of his long ride. He turned when the door of the office was opened, and nodded at Harper, who paused in the office doorway with expectancy showing on his face.

'Howdy, Brad? Has it been quiet around here? I had my trip for nothing. Jim Tolliver wasn't around when I got to his place, and Hickman said Tolliver was lying dead in his yard. I did see a patch of blood there but no body. It's a mystery, and I haven't been able think of an answer. My guess is that Tolliver wasn't dead, but in that case he would have come to town if he'd been shot. The only other explanation is that whoever killed him went back and removed the body after Hickman had seen it. Perhaps Hickman riding in disturbed the killer and he hid up until Hickman had gone.'

'That seems the likely explanation,' Harper agreed. 'But you've got a lot more to worry about here, Mort.'

Bland's expression hardened as he listened to Harper's account of the incidents which had occurred during his absence. When Harper lapsed into silence Bland lifted his hands chest high, then let them fall back to his sides.

'Hell, Brad, what is going on around here?' he demanded.

'All I know is that those men who came to town to set up the sawmill are responsible for most of the trouble so far. Out at Benton's place a man named Norton Calder and a gunman called Badger drew on me for no reason at all. Calder is the manager of the sawmill. Then Shreeve and Buster, both saw-yers, set a gun trap for me in the stable. And when I went to the sawmill this morning four men pulled guns on me. I've got three of them in the cells. The other one is ready for boot hill.'

'And Redfern is lying dead in Archer's barn!' Bland mused, shaking his head. 'I guess I'd better get to work. I'll have the truth out of the prisoners if it takes all day. What do you think you should do, Brad? You know more about what's been going on than I do, so I'll leave it to you to follow your own inclination.'

'I need to pick up Frank Benton again,' Harper said, 'and catch Norton Calder. He's apparently the kingpin in this business and I've got a lot of questions to ask him.'

'OK. Get on with that and I'll handle the town. I'll have to keep some of the posse men on duty until you get back.'

'Watch your back at all times,' Harper warned. 'It looks like someone is out to get rid of the law in this county.'

'I'll be ready for them,' Bland responded.

Harper turned to Bob Fuller, who was seated beside Lily-Beth at the sheriff's desk.

'What are your plans, Bob?' Harper demanded.

'I'd like to ride with you in case you meet up with Benton again,' Fuller said earnestly.

'And what about Lily?' Harper shook his head. 'She should come first in your thinking. I know Benton said the deal about your spread had changed and he was no longer interested in it, but are you going to take his word for it?'

'Heck, no, I can't do that!' Fuller shook his head. 'Put it like that and I know what I've got to do. We'll stay in town until you've picked up the men you're after. It wouldn't do for us to fall into Benton's hands again.'

'That's better.' Harper drew his pistol and checked it. 'I'm riding out now, and I won't be back until I've picked up at least one of the men I want. Stay close to Bob, Lily. Just remember what happened to you the last time.'

The girl suppressed a shiver and nodded emphatically. Harper departed, sighing with relief as he walked along the street to the livery barn to get his horse. On an afterthought he turned back to the general store for some spare shells.

Sim Archer was standing behind his counter talking to a couple of townsmen. Harper did not need to be told what was being discussed: Redfern's body in the barn out back. In the past there had never been much trouble around Clear Spring and this lawlessness was hitting the town hard.

'I saw Mort riding in a while ago,' Archer said. 'What's he going to do about that stiff in my barn?'

'Give him time,' Harper advised. 'He's up to his neck in it right now.'

'You arrested some of those men at the new sawmill,' Archer continued. 'Are they mixed up in this trouble?'

'We're not sure yet, but it will all come out before it's over. Give me a box of .45s and a box of .44-.40s. I'm riding out to pick up a couple of men.'

Archer handed over the boxes of cartridges and Harper took his leave. He reached the end of the sidewalk and started to cross to the livery barn when a thought struck him. He turned to the back lots to visit the sawmill. He loosened his pistol in its holster as he reached the big front door and peered inside. The interior was still and looked strangely defunct. He entered and walked around, but there was nothing to hold his attention and he went on to the stable.

He entered the livery barn by the back door, mindful of the gun trap which had been set for him during the night, but had no trouble getting his buckskin. He saddled up and rode out, settling himself to cover the distance to the Benton ranch and hoping that his luck would change and he could arrest at least one of the men he wanted.

Harper felt a weight lift from his mind as he cleared the town and headed across open range. He decided to look in at the Fuller place before going on to the trading post, in case Dack Hoose had returned; then he planned to check out Benton's spread. It was early afternoon when he reined in on a rise overlooking the Bar F, and he shook his head at the sight of the blackened ruins of the ranch house. The barn looked deserted but he took no chances as he rode in, and his right hand was close to the butt of his holstered pistol.

The buckskin's hoofs rattled on the hard ground as he crossed the yard. He was ten yards from the big door of the building when a man stepped into view from inside and paused. He was holding a Winchester in his hands and regarded Harper stolidly. Harper reined in and sat motionless, the fingers of his right hand resting lightly on the butt of his pistol.

'Who are you and what are you doing here?' Harper demanded.

'Before you get uppity, Deputy, take a look to your right,' the man replied. 'I got a sidekick at that corner and he's covering you.'

Harper glimpsed a slight movement from a corner of his eye and flicked a glance in that direction to see a man easing forward into view at the right-hand corner of the barn. He recognized the man instantly; he had been arrested out at Benton's place, and was one of the men who had been busted out of jail.

'It's the deputy who arrested us,' the man said gleefully. 'Benton will be pleased to see him. OK, Deputy, put your hands up or I'll shoot you out of your saddle.'

'Not so fast,' Harper replied without hesitation. 'You don't think I was stupid enough to ride in here alone, do you? I've got a twenty-man posse surrounding this place, and if you don't throw down your guns and raise your hands they will start shooting like it is the Civil War all over again.'

'You're bluffing,' the man replied, but nevertheless he threw a searching glance around the yard. 'You get your hands up and we'll take a ride to Benton's place. He'll know what to do with you.'

'There's a second posse heading to

176

Benton's place,' Harper said. 'They should be picking up Benton just about now, if he was foolish enough to return to his spread.'

'I told you it was stupid to come in here and wait for the Fullers to show up again,' said the man in the doorway. 'We should have got clear of the county after opening the jail.'

'So you were one of the two men who busted my prisoners out of jail!' Harper regarded the man steadily. 'How did you get Redfern to open the door of the office, and who killed him afterwards and put his body in the barn back of the general store?'

The man remained silent, gazing at Harper with narrowed eyes.

'OK.' Harper glanced around as if looking for his posse men. 'You've had long enough to consider my ultimatum. Now you better throw down your guns or get blasted.'

'I ain't falling for that,' said the man at the corner of the barn.

'He could be telling the truth,' the

other countered, 'and I ain't gonna take a chance. He wouldn't have ridden in here alone. I've been feeling uneasy all morning.' He threw his rifle to the ground and raised his hands. 'OK, I quit,' he said. 'Tell the posse not to shoot.'

'You crazy fool!' yelled the other. 'Pick up your gun, Turner. He's bluffing, I tell you.'

Harper saw Turner glance towards his sidekick, then bend to retrieve his rifle. Harper set his gun hand into motion. He drew his pistol and cocked it before Turner was aware of the movement and, when Turner jerked up at the sound of the pistol being cocked, Harper squeezed his trigger, aiming for Turner's right shoulder. The crash of the shot blasted the silence into shreds and Turner jumped when the bullet struck him. He fell back against the corner of the barn. His rifle dropped from his hands before he twisted and fell inertly on to his face.

Harper covered the other man, who

seemed stunned by the sudden turn of events.

'You've got more sense,' Harper observed, 'so keep using it. Get rid of that pistol in your holster and throw down any other weapons you have on you. Then take a look at your pard. He ain't dead yet so we'll patch him up before I decide what to do with you.'

'Where's your posse?' the man demanded.

'They are still in town.' Harper smiled.

The man's face changed expression. 'Listen, I'll do a deal with you,' he said earnestly. 'I didn't like this game when I first came to it, and what's happened since has proved me right. I want out, and this is a good time to skedaddle. I ain't shot anyone or broke the law around here.'

'I'll think about it.' Harper motioned with his pistol. 'Get moving. You're wasting my time.'

The man went to Turner's side and bent over him. When he straightened he was shaking his head.

'You shoot too straight,' he observed. 'It looks like you hit him in the lung. I don't reckon he's got long to live.'

'Move away and I'll take a look at him,' Harper directed.

He waited until the man had stepped back several yards before dismounting and trailing his reins. He crossed to where Turner was lying and dropped to one knee beside the inert figure. A glance was enough to inform him that Turner was about to cash his chips. He saw the man's eyelids flicker, then open. Turner looked up at him.

'You've done for me, Deputy,' he accused. 'I've come to the end of my trail.'

Harper nodded. 'No sense in denying it,' he said. 'Is there anyone I can inform about you?'

'Not a soul,' Turner whispered, and closed his eyes. Blood flecked his thin lips, and then a sudden gush came from his mouth and a tremor shook him. He groaned, and as the sound faded he relaxed in death.

Harper arose, blotting his emotions. He looked around, checking his surroundings, and spotted an approaching haze of dust on the range. He watched it for several moments, until four riders took shape within the grey shroud, and then glanced at his watchful prisoner.

'We'd better get out of here but quick,' Harper said. 'Where's your horse?'

'It's in the barn. You ain't got a chance of getting clear. That'll be some more of the gang coming in. We were told to expect them.'

'Shut up and get moving. I'll do a deal with you, so let's ride. Whatever is going on around here, the law can't be beaten, so you're the one with no chance.'

The prisoner studied the four riders before turning to enter the barn. Harper followed him closely, and took a rifle from the man's saddle scabbard. He followed the man when the horse was led out of the barn and they mounted.

'Let's head off behind the barn,' Harper directed. 'I'm going to visit Benton's spread.'

'You'll be riding into trouble if you go there,' the man warned. 'You don't need me along so let us do a deal now and I'll head for other parts.'

'This ain't the time for dealing,' Harper told him. 'Do you know those four riders?'

'They are too far off right now to make out details, but I expect they are coming to relieve Turner and me.'

'So hit the trail and we'll give them the slip. Then we'll do a deal.'

The man shrugged and fed steel to his mount. The horse jumped forward and hit a gallop within a few strides. They circled the barn and headed out fast across the range. When they reached the nearest rise Harper glanced back and saw three of the riders swinging round the barn to follow at a gallop. He grimaced when he realized that he was in trouble, and eased away from his prisoner in case the man should get any ideas about resisting. But the man seemed eager now to get clear, and urged his horse on to even greater effort.

As they dropped down beyond the rise to continue, a fusillade of shots rang out. Harper ducked as flying lead buzzed around them like a swarm of angry hornets. He was aware that this was a time to run not fight.

8

Harper looked around for a spot from which to fight but was hampered by his prisoner's presence. He needed to render the man helpless before attempting to deal with the newcomers, and kept urging him on. The gunman seemed eager to keep clear of trouble and stayed just ahead of Harper as they headed out across the range. The trio at their backs followed recklessly, shooting whenever they figured to score hits.

The undulating range aided Harper's efforts to get clear. For most of the time they were out of sight of their pursuers, and the pursuers could get only fleeting shots at them. But Harper realized he could not pull away, and watched for a suitable ambush spot from which to discourage the trio. He was familiar with the range, and angled to the east until he arrived at a stretch of broken ground. The pursuers were well behind but still determined to get to grips.

'Pull up and get off your horse,' Harper said at length. 'Drop into that depression over there and keep your head down. I'll be a few yards behind you, so don't try to get away.'

The man swung out of his saddle and dived into the depression that Harper had indicated. Harper led both horses up a rise in the ground to a sprawl of copper-coloured rocks on a low crest, where he dismounted. He drew his Winchester and took spare shells from a saddle-bag before dropping into a firing position behind the rocks. The prisoner was down in his position, and Harper kept an eye on the spot as he looked around.

The three riders came into view, pushing their mounts hard. Harper jacked a cartridge into his breech and squinted through his sights. The three men were strangers, but they had made their intention plain. He waited for them to draw within range.

He drew a bead on the centre man of the trio and fired. The flat crack of the rifle sent echoes across the range and gunsmoke flared. The rider jerked, then twisted to fall from his saddle. He thumped the ground hard and remained motionless. The two remaining riders swerved their mounts to hunt for cover. Harper let them go. When they disappeared over a ridge he got to his feet and called the prisoner to join him.

'Did you kill him?' the gun man asked.

Harper shrugged. 'Probably, but I don't have time to check him out. His sidekicks will look him over after we've gone. Mount up and let's push on.'

'What about my deal?'

Harper glanced around. He expected the two surviving riders to circle around his position and sneak up from the rear, and felt an urgent need to get moving.

'We'll talk later and I'll see if you've got anything worth dealing with,' he said. 'If you know something that I don't then we'll dicker, but if you've got nothing then you'll wind up in the jail in Clear Spring.'

The man grimaced and stepped up into his saddle. They went on, and Harper angled into a different direction. He watched their back trail. He saw nothing more of their pursuers but did not doubt that they were still following. He was aware that he could not go on to the Benton place with a couple of hostile men on his back trail.

'We'll hold up here for a spell,' Harper called when he saw a spot which was suitable for defence.

They dismounted on rock-strewn high ground and Harper produced handcuffs which he clicked around the man's wrists.

'Just stay quiet and still and you might come out of this ahead of the game,' Harper said. 'I want to know if we are still being followed.'

The man shrugged but made no comment. He dropped to the ground and remained motionless. Harper drew his rifle and got down behind a mound.

He removed his Stetson and lay watching his back trail. The silence was intense and nothing moved anywhere within his field of vision. The sun was hot on his back and he was thirsty but remained motionless. He reckoned that he was several miles from the trading post. He decided to visit it before concentrating on catching Frank Benton, for Dack Hoose was involved in this crooked game, and Harper did not intend that the trader should escape the law.

While he waited he considered the situation which had developed since Bob Fuller was abducted. He realized that Norton Calder was the kingpin in the crooked game being played. Apparently Calder had not returned to town after their confrontation at the Benton place. He wondered where the man was holed up.

Harper waited for an hour without sighting any movement on his back trail. He checked his surroundings constantly, aware that the gun men pursuing him would no longer make a frontal approach. When he was satisfied that he was in the clear he decided to move on. He turned to his docile prisoner, who was apparently dozing to while away the time.

'So what have you got to make a deal with?' he demanded.

The man stirred and sat up. He glanced around before lifting his manacled hands.

'Take these off and then I'll talk,' he said.

Harper grinned. 'Those cuffs are around your wrists, not your tongue,' he replied. 'Quit stalling and start talking.'

'A man named Norton Calder is bossing the crooked deal to steal range in this county. He did the same thing east of here last year and got away with it.'

'I know about Calder.' Harper shook his head. 'You'll have to do better than that. I met up with Calder at Benton's place and killed his sidekick, a man called Badger. Calder took out at a run and I haven't set eyes on him since.'

'*You* killed Badger?' The man's expression changed. 'I saw him lying dead in Benton's yard when I passed through there early this morning. Say, Badger was Calder's top gun!'

'So what else do you know?' Harper persisted.

'Calder ain't the top man. There is a guy by the name of Stross — Reuben Stross, who lives back East and finances Calder. He's the guy you have to put out of business to stop this crooked game.'

'Where does he live? Stross was mentioned at the Benton place but there were no other details beyond his name.'

'I don't know anything more about him. I heard Calder talking about Stross, that's all, but he'll be showing up around here any day now because he likes to be in at the kill. There is also another man who's in on this crooked deal. I don't know where he hangs out but he's got a lot of say, and I heard him giving Calder orders. He lives in the county. I did hear Calder call him Buck a couple of times, and once he called him Chilvers. He was at Benton's place last night and talked to Calder. I heard him but couldn't see him in the dark. He chewed up Calder considerable for failing to get rid of you, and was put out because you showed up in town with prisoners and he had to arrange for them to be busted out of jail. He rode off before I got a chance to learn anything more about him.'

'Is he a local man?' Harper demanded.

'I guess so.' The prisoner shrugged. 'He spoke like he knew Stross personal, and hinted to Calder that he could be tossed out on his ear for failing to keep to their schedule.'

'Buck Chilvers,' Harper mused, and shook his head. 'I ain't ever come across that name. Are you giving it to me straight?'

'I swear to God!' The man nodded fervently. 'And that's about all I can tell you. There's big trouble coming to this county and you don't have enough lawmen to beat it. By the time you wake up to that fact it will all be over and this range will belong to Stross and Calder. I want out because the scheme is too big for me. I don't see them getting away with it again. They were lucky the last time, but this is different. You've put a crimp in their plans and they ain't got moving like they should.'

'What can you tell me about Dack Hoose?' Harper urged. 'I know he's involved with the gang.'

'Hoose knew Stross and Calder twenty years ago down in Texas, where Stross made his money. And I got a feeling that Buck Chilvers was with the Texas gang in those days. Calder saw Hoose at the trading post on his first look around the county and Hoose threw in his lot with them. Now, how about turning me loose? The sooner I shake the dust of this range off my boots the better I'll like it.'

Harper reached into his pocket for the key to the cuffs. 'When you ride out of here I don't wanta see your face again,' he said. He tossed over the key, then covered the man with his pistol. 'If you don't quit this range I'll shoot you on sight the next time I set eyes on you.'

'You won't see me again.' The man freed himself, tossed the cuffs in front of Harper, then flipped the key beside them. 'Can I have my gun back?' he asked.

'The hell you can! Go on, get out of here before I change my mind. I wouldn't turn you loose except you'll hamper me when I go for Benton. Get on your horse and don't stop riding until you're clear of this county.'

The man grinned and got to his feet. He turned to go to his horse, hidden in nearby rocks, then he uttered a shocked cry and pitched forward on to his face. Harper heard the sickening smack of a bullet as it struck the man, and the crash of a gun threw echoes across the range. For a moment Harper gazed at the motionless figure. He could see a bullet hole in the back of the man's shirt, and blood was soaking quickly into the surrounding material.

Fighting his shock, Harper threw himself to his left, his gun lifting, his gaze sweeping his surroundings. He caught a glimpse of furtive movement to his left, saw a figure rising up from behind a rock, and fired instantly. A quick movement to his right as a second man reared up caught his eye and he hurled himself into cover as two bullets smacked rock near his head. Splinters slashed his right cheek. He fell heavily, twisted on to his back, and swung his gun to cover the attack. A hand was lifting above a rock to point a pistol at him and he fired again, aiming for the hand.

The blasting shots hammered through the stillness. Harper's bullet struck the hand and the gun dropped to the ground. A bearded face came into view, and the man's left hand, gripping a pistol, also appeared. Harper triggered his gun and a red splotch appeared between the man's eyes. He was thrown backwards by the impact of the slug and disappeared behind the rock as gun echoes faded.

Harper thrust himself to his feet and lunged forward, his gaze sweeping the surrounding area. Silence was returning, the echoes of the shooting sounding hollow in the distance. He recognized the nearest man as one of the trio that had followed his trail from the Fuller ranch; now all three were down. He strode to where the second man was crumpled on the ground and turned him over to check that he was dead. Satisfied, he returned to his erstwhile prisoner. He shook his head as he looked down at the man's stiffening face.

Fetching his buckskin, Harper turned the other horse loose, then followed boot tracks to where the horses of the two ambushers were standing in cover. He turned both animals loose before riding on in the direction of the trading post, his thoughts occupied by the information he had been given. He did not doubt the veracity of what he had been told.

He needed to take live prisoners now, he thought. He was shooting his way through the opposition, but the law demanded proof of wrongdoing and he would have to justify his actions if he survived to complete his investigation. His duty was plain. He wanted to take Hoose, Benton and Calder alive to gain more information about the plot to steal range. Impatience prickled in the back of his mind as he continued.

The trading post was silent and still when Harper reached an overlooking ridge. He reined in to study the place. The two posse men were still lying out front, and he frowned as he regarded their bodies. From what he knew of Dack Hoose he doubted that the man had fled, especially as he was involved with the land steal.

He set out to circle the post, remaining in cover as he looked for tracks which would give him an idea of the activity that had taken place since his last visit. When he came across several sets of tracks, some heading into

196

the post and others going in the opposite direction, he dismounted and examined them closely to discover that all had been made by the same horse. He nodded, certain that Hoose had not fled, and if he was reading the hoofprints correctly then Hoose was in the post right now, for the horse had ridden in three times during the past twenty-four hours and had departed only twice.

Harper checked his pistol and continued circling until he returned to the spot from where he started. He dismounted and edged forward to the crest of the ridge to observe the one-storey building. The trading post was still: silent like boot hill on a wet Sunday afternoon. He decided to ride in and flush Hoose out — if it was the trader who had left the tracks. He swung into his saddle and began the approach, his right hand close to his holstered pistol.

He managed to keep some scrub between himself and the post as he approached, but it was poor cover, and he was not surprised when a bullet clipped a twig beside his head before he had covered many yards. The flat echoes of a rifle shot cracked the silence. He dismounted quickly and drew his Winchester from its scabbard. The long gun fired several more shots in his direction before falling silent, then when he heard the rattle of hoofs on hard ground, he ran forward to get a look at the departing rider.

Hoose was in the saddle of a bay horse and heading for the distant hills at a breakneck pace. Harper lifted his rifle and took aim at the fleeing man. He fired two shots, and a moment later the bay went down in a heavy fall. Hoose hit the ground hard and remained motionless when he came to rest. Harper cuffed sweat from his forehead and fetched his buckskin to ride over to where Hoose was trying to rise. He checked Hoose's horse, found it was dead, and went to the trader.

'You made a bad mistake sticking

around here, Hoose,' Harper observed. He bent over the big man. Blood was trickling from a bullet wound in Hoose's left shoulder, but the trader was making more fuss about his right leg.

'Damn you! My leg is busted,' Hoose snarled. 'What for did you have to turn up at this moment? I was clearing out this time. Now I ain't going anywhere.'

'Except to jail,' Harper retorted. He pulled a knife from a sheath on his belt and slit open the right leg of Hoose's pants. 'You ain't gonna be walking anywhere for weeks,' he observed. 'The leg sure is busted — the shinbone is sticking out through the flesh. So you threw in with the land stealers, huh? But you're out of it now.'

'Who told you that?' Hoose demanded through gritted teeth. 'Heck, I'm just an honest trader trying to make a living in this god-forsaken hole!'

'Fill me in on details about Calder and Stross which I don't have,' Harper cut in.

'I got nothing to say to you,' Hoose growled.

'Suit yourself. I've got a lot to do before I can think about returning to town so you'll have to lie here and wait for me to get back. I could make you comfortable before I leave, but if you're not gonna help me then I'm damned if I'll do anything for you. I reckon I'll be gone about twenty-four hours, and in that time it is likely your leg will turn bad. It's in real bad shape. So you have a choice, Hoose. Open up and I'll tend to you, or keep your trap shut and you'll die out here before tomorrow comes.'

'What do you wanta know?' Hoose narrowed his shifty eyes and glared at Harper.

'I thought you'd see it my way.' Harper grinned humourlessly. 'You ain't so tough, Hoose! Just answer one question and I'll help you.'

'I asked you what you want, so get on with it,' Hoose snarled.

'Who is Buck Chilvers?'

'Buck Chilvers!' Surprise showed momentarily on Hoose's sweating face. 'I never heard of him!'

'You rode with a gang that operated in Texas about twenty years ago,' Harper continued. 'Calder was in that gang and so were Reuben Stross and Buck Chilvers.'

'If you know so much about that deal then how come you don't know about Chilvers?' Hoose demanded. 'Anyway, I heard years ago that Buck died down on the Mexican border in a gunfight with Texas Rangers.'

'Maybe that was what he wanted folks to believe,' Harper said. 'My information is that he is alive and living around here. Describe him as he looked when you saw him last.'

'Hell, I didn't recognize Calder when he walked into the trading post a month ago.' Hoose shook his head. 'Even when he told me his real name — the one he used in Texas — I couldn't place him. We were all young in those days and still had some growing to do after we parted. So don't ask me about Chilvers. I wouldn't know him from Adam.'

'OK!' Harper straightened. 'You stick to that and I'll be on my way. I'll look in on you when I head back to town tomorrow. Maybe you'll feel more like helping me then — if you're still alive.'

He went to his buckskin and swung into the saddle. Hoose watched him with disbelief showing on his contorted face. Harper shook his reins and the buckskin moved on.

'Hey, you can't leave me lying here!' Hoose shouted.

'I don't want to,' Harper replied, 'but you leave me no choice. Like I said, I'll drop in tomorrow to see how you're making out.'

Hoose made no reply and Harper kept riding, heading in the direction of the Benton spread. The afternoon was wearing away and he wanted to reach the ranch just after sundown. Then Hoose called to him. He reined in, then turned back, grinning at the desperation showing on Hoose's sweaty face.

'I just remembered something about Buck Chilvers that should put you on his trail,' Hoose said. 'He lost the little finger off his left hand when a bank job went wrong and he was too close to the dynamite when it exploded. All you've got to do is look for a man with a missing finger. So how about fixing me up before you ride on?'

'Sure. I'll do what I can for you. I'll be able to come back to you if I find you're a liar, because you ain't gonna be up and about for weeks.'

'You've got the straight of it,' Hoose insisted. 'Put me in the trading post and I'll be OK.'

Harper lifted Hoose across the saddle of the buckskin despite the man's cries of agony and took him into the trading post. He tended Hoose's wounds and made him comfortable on his bed with water and food close to hand, and a bottle of whiskey.

'That's the best I can do for you,' Harper said when he'd finished. 'Some-one might drop in while I'm away and you could send him to town for the doctor. I'll do the same if I meet anyone on the range. I'll be back tomorrow in any case.'

'And if you get yourself killed in the meantime?' Hoose demanded. 'I'll lie here until I rot.'

'That'll be your hard luck,' Harper retorted.

'No,' a voice rasped from a corner of the store. 'It's your hard luck that Hoose let me stay here, Harper. I've been waiting for you to finish tending him. Now get your hands up.'

Harper glanced over his shoulder and saw Joss Kemp leaning beside a stack of crates. The ex-deputy was holding a pistol in his hand.

'So this is where you ended up,' Harper observed. 'I would have thought you'd high-tail it out of the county. You wouldn't be safe within a hundred miles of here.'

'I couldn't leave after taking a slug from you,' Kemp snarled. 'I knew you'd be out prowling around, but I didn't think you'd walk in here like a steer heading for the slaughterhouse. I was watching from a window when you rode up.' He glanced at Hoose. 'At one time it didn't look like you would get him to bring you in here under my gun, Hoose.'

'I did a deal with him,' Hoose replied, grinning despite his pain. 'He was asking about Buck Chilvers and I gave him some guff about Chilvers missing a little finger off his left hand. He fell for it, and here we are. Are you gonna kill him, Kemp?'

'That's the plan, but I reckon Benton will want to talk to him first so I'll take him over to the ranch. My bet is that Harper ain't made a report yet about what happened at the Benton place, so if he dies now no one will know what really happened there, and I can go back to town as a deputy.'

'No chance,' Harper said. 'I spread the word about you soon as I hit Main Street. There ain't a man in town who doesn't know you're a renegade.'

'You would say that, but I can twist the facts to suit my story. Now get your hands up. You can try and make a play if you fancy your chance. I'll be only too happy to send you to hell.'

Harper shook his head and kept his hands clear of his waist. Kemp was a cold-blooded killer, but he looked as if he were in the grip of a fever. The bullet wound in his shoulder which Harper had given him at Benton's spread was taking its toll. Kemp's eyes were glassy and he was sweating profusely. The escape from jail had been a wrong move for him, and now he was paying the price. Harper began to feel a pang of hope. With any luck Kemp would fall out of his saddle before they reached the Benton ranch.

But Kemp did not display any weakness as he disarmed Harper. He stayed out of arm's reach until Harper was defenceless, then he stepped in close behind and slammed his pistol barrel against Harper's head. Harper folded without a sound as blackness filled his mind. He was unconscious before he hit the floor, and did not feel the kicking Kemp gave him. Hoose watched impassively, enjoying the punishment, but eventually called to Kemp to desist.

'Benton will want to talk to him so don't kick his lights out,' Hoose suggested.

Kemp leaned against a stack of crates, breathless and unsteady. His exertions had raised his fever to a higher level and he was now feeling unwell. His senses were gyrating, there were black specks before his eyes, and he was hard put to maintain his balance. But he gripped his gun and covered Harper as if expecting him to spring up and fight.

'By the look of you I'd say you ain't gonna make it to Benton's place today,' Hoose observed. 'You better hit the sack in the back room until you're feeling better. You've got a fever, Kemp, in case you don't know it, so hogtie Harper and give me a gun to keep him down when he comes back to his senses.'

Kemp bent to pick up Harper's pistol, overbalanced, and fell to the floor on his hands and knees. He shook his head slowly as he threw Harper's gun to where Hoose was lying, and fell on his face as the trader scooped up the weapon. Hoose cocked the gun and aimed it at Harper, For a moment he hesitated, with the impulse to kill vibrating in his mind. Then common sense prevailed and he lowered the weapon, aware that he could kill the deputy at any time, but he fancied having some fun with Harper before finishing him off.

9

Harper was disturbed by the sound of someone groaning. He opened his eyes and realized that he was making the noise. A crushing pain had taken up lodgings in his head in response to the blow he had received from Kemp's pistol, and when he moved convulsively he discovered that his body was occupied by darting pangs of agony which flared through him at the slightest movement. His ribs felt as if some had been broken. A large area around his stomach protested with a deep throbbing pain, making him wonder whether he had been kicked by a mule. A similar patch of deep-seated agony around his kidneys protested painfully at his slightest movement, and he guessed that Kemp had worked him over after he had fallen unconscious.

He lifted his head and his senses

swirled. He stifled a groan as he raised a hand to his aching skull. Each movement filled him with protesting agony but he forced his eyes to remain open and looked around. He was lying on the floor of the trading post, almost in the doorway that led into Hoose's private quarters. Shadows were filling the big room and the black smears of approaching night were pressing against the dusty windowpanes. He looked for Kemp but saw no sign of the crooked ex-deputy.

'Kemp is out cold, Harper,' Hoose called from the shadows of the inner room. 'I got the upper hand now, and I'm holding a gun on you. Get up, but slow. Any attempt to get away will bring you a bullet. I owe you a slug in the guts for breaking my leg, so go easy.'

Harper looked into the room where he had laid Hoose down but saw little more than an outline of the trader lying on the bunk.

'I can see you plain,' Hoose called, 'and I've got my sights on you. This time you ain't getting away. Get up and light a lamp. There's one in here. Strike a match and let me take a look at you. Kemp sure gave you a good kicking, and I'm sorry I didn't get the chance to put the boot in.'

'Where is Kemp?' Harper demanded.

'He's in my guest room.' Hoose laughed hoarsely. 'The damn fool is full of fever from that slug you put in him. It's a good thing you turned up when you did. An hour later and Kemp would have been out like a babe full of mother's milk. Now get moving before I lose my patience and shoot you.'

Harper eased on to his left side and pressed a hand to the floor. When he began to lever himself upright he discovered pain in muscles he had not been aware he possessed. He groaned and fell back, and heard Hoose laugh.

'This is the first time you've had a good kicking, huh?' Hoose snarled. 'I hope it's hurting you real good, but it's nothing to what you'll get when Kemp is back on his feet. You're in for a humdinger of a beating, and I'll enjoy every minute of it. Now get that lamp burning before I have to shoot you to make sure of you. Much as I'd like to gut-shoot you, I'd rather wait for your kick-off and watch you squirm before you go.'

Harper made another effort to get to his feet. He smothered his groans as each movement filled him with agony. Sweat ran down his face. His senses swirled. He was shaky inside. He staggered, almost fell, and leaned against the doorpost to retain his balance. He reached into a breast pocket, found a match, and scratched it on the post. When it flared he held it up and looked around. He saw a lamp on an adjacent table and crossed to it. He lit the lamp and turned up the wick until bright yellow light flooded the room. He saw Hoose propped up on the bunk, holding a pistol pointed in his direction.

'You can put the gun away,' Harper said. 'You won't shoot me because I'm your only hope of getting out of here alive.'

'I'll take my chance on someone showing up before long,' Hoose replied. 'You're too sure I won't shoot, but, brother, you're teetering on the edge of hell right now.'

Harper lifted a hand to his head. He could feel dried blood in his hair and on his face.

'You shoulda killed Kemp when you had the chance,' Hoose said.

'Maybe I should have killed you while I was at it. Do like I say, Hoose. Throw down that gun. You're not looking too good and I'm the only one can help you. Think on it. If I ain't around then you're in mighty bad trouble.'

'No dice! Kemp's handcuffs are lying on that chair. Put them on your wrists with your hands either side of that post by the window. That should hold you for the night, and I'll feel easier with you helpless.'

Harper saw the handcuffs and went forward to pick them up. Hoose followed his movement with the pistol. The black hole of the muzzle seemed to gape larger when Harper looked into it, and Hoose laughed.

'It ain't a pretty sight, huh? No joke being on the wrong end of a gun, is it? Now get those cuffs on quick or you'll be lying on the floor with an extra eye in your forehead. I'm getting mighty tired of standing you off. I need some sleep, and I can't do that with you standing there.'

Harper staggered and dropped to one knee, aware that if he obeyed Hoose he would be finished. Hoose jerked up at his movement, following Harper with the gun, and cursed when pain stabbed through his broken leg.

'What the hell are you trying to pull?' Hoose demanded. 'You're asking for a bullet.'

Harper did not reply. He closed his eyes as if losing his senses, and dropped his chin to his chest.

Hoose chuckled. 'Kemp sure gave you a good going over,' he observed.

Harper peered at the trader through

narrowed eyes. The pistol in Hoose's hand wavered slightly and Harper tensed himself to act. He ignored the pain stabbing through his body and hurled the handcuffs into Hoose's face, at the same time thrusting himself flat to the floor. The pistol exploded instantly and a burning pain, swift as a flash of lightning, darted across the top of Harper's left shoulder but missed his vital points. Harper was unable to believe his luck.

The thunder of the shot almost deafened Harper in the close confines of the room. Ignoring his pain, he lunged forward to grapple with Hoose, who was trying to bring his pistol to bear. Harper's right hand closed around the barrel of the gun and he exerted his strength in a twisting movement. Hoose lost his grip on the weapon. Harper reversed the pistol and stuck the muzzle against Hoose's left thigh.

'Ease up or I'll cripple you permanent,' Harper said through clenched teeth.

Hoose slumped on the bunk. Harper pushed himself gingerly to his feet. He picked up the handcuffs. Blood was trickling from Hoose's face where the cuffs had caught him.

'Don't give me any more trouble, Hoose,' Harper warned. 'I've wasted too much time on you already.'

He checked the gun, saw that it was his own pistol, and thrust it into his holster. He searched Hoose for other weapons, found a long-bladed knife, and tossed it across the room. He searched the area of the bunk but found nothing else.

'Where did you say Kemp is?' Harper demanded.

'He's in the back room, through that door. He'll be dead to the world right now. He's got a fever.'

'I wouldn't trust Kemp if he was hogtied.' Harper took the handcuffs along, crossed to the door, and peered into a small room. Joss Kemp was sprawled on a mattress on the floor in a corner with a pistol beside him; he was either asleep or unconscious. Harper picked up the gun and stuck it in his waistband. He cuffed Kemp's wrists together and left him lying, out to the world.

'He'll keep until tomorrow,' Harper observed when he returned to Hoose. 'I'm pulling out now, and you better hope I make it through the next few hours. I'm going to pick up the prisoners who escaped from the jail in town, and I want to locate Buck Chilvers, whoever he is. You just stay quiet here, Hoose, and I'll be back for you tomorrow.'

Hoose cursed as Harper departed. Harper went for his buckskin. The night had settled on the range and dense shadows clung to the ground. Relief filled Harper as he rode away from the trading post, but he soon discovered that the jolting saddle filled him with great discomfort. He continued although his instinct was to stop and rest, perhaps to sleep through the night before continuing, but he ignored the impulse.

He had a job to do, and while he could stand and fight nothing would keep him from it.

His condition seemed to ease a fraction as he persevered. He rode towards the Benton spread, picking his direction unerringly through the night. He kept his ears strained for sound but heard nothing beyond the natural noises of the range. Time seemed to be of no importance during that ride and he had to call upon all his reserves of determination and willpower to continue. Throbbing pain in his body was a constant reminder of the tough life he led, and he slipped into a reverie which was punctuated by the agonies of his discomfort.

He surmised that he was getting close to the Benton ranch but could see nothing in the wide expanse of rangeland. When he heard the faint drumming of hoofs on the hard ground ahead he did not at first recognize it for what it was and kept riding forward. Then a shot was fired. He saw the flash and heard the whine of a speeding bullet passing over his head. He almost fell out of his saddle in his haste to dismount, but realized instantly that he was not the target. More shots slammed the silence. Harper drew his pistol and stood waiting for developments.

The sound of an approaching horse grew louder. Soon he could make out the shapeless mass of a rider hunched over in a saddle and working hard to get the best possible speed from his mount. A pursuing gun blasted three shots, and Harper heard the passage of hot lead crackling through the shadows. The fleeing rider passed Harper closely, anonymous in the gloom. The chasing gun fired again, then the pursuer loomed up, galloped by only yards from Harper's position, and vanished into the night.

Harper climbed back into his saddle and swung his horse, ignoring his pain as he took out in pursuit. He could hear the two galloping horses plainly, and urged the buckskin into its best speed.

The pistol hammered from time to time, and flashes split the dense shadows. Harper gained on the riders. He held his pistol ready in his right hand, his eyes narrowed to pierce the shadows, but he could see little and had to use his ears in order to stay on the trail of his quarry.

The pistol hammered again. Harper heard a cry, then the sound of a horse going down in midstride. He pulled on his reins to slow the buckskin, peering ahead for movement. The next instant his mount almost slammed into a horse which had halted. He caught sight of a shapeless blur as the buckskin narrowly avoided a collision, then a harsh cry split the heavier sound of hoofs and Harper glimpsed a man, afoot, trying to get out from under the buckskin's lunging mass. Harper's horse struck the man, sent him flying, then almost went down. It twisted to stay on its feet, and Harper went out of the saddle sideways. He hit the ground hard.

The impact winded him and he

remained helpless for several moments. He could hear a horse just ahead, and knew by the noise it was making that it had been injured. He discovered that he was still holding his pistol, and began to make tentative movements to check himself for additional injuries. At last he got to his feet and looked around. The man who had been doing all the shooting was lying huddled on the grass just behind him. Harper approached the inert figure with caution. The man was unconscious, breathing shallowly, and a pistol glinted in the starlight, close to his side.

Harper picked up the gun and turned to approach the injured horse which had been ridden by the fleeing rider. The animal was trying to rise. Harper tried to make out details, wondering where the rider was, and at that moment a woman's voice called out, ragged with shock.

'OK, I've had enough. I'll go along with you.'

'Lily-Beth, is that you?' Harper

demanded, shocked because he thought he recognized her voice.

'Brad! Thank God!' Lily-Beth materialized out of the dense shadows. She staggered, and Harper caught her as she began to fall. He could not see her face in the faint starshine.

'Jeez, what are you doing out here?' he demanded. 'And who was chasing you?'

'I don't know,' she replied wearily. Her tone was high-pitched, racked with shock and fright. 'I was taken off the street in town this afternoon by two men, and no one did anything to help me although there were folks around. Sheriff Bland came out of the law office as we were passing. I called out to him and one of the men shot him in cold blood. I don't know if he was killed, but he fell and was still. The two men were strangers, and they said nothing during the ride, but it looked like they were heading for the Benton place. When sundown came I swung my mount into one of them and fled. The other man chased me, and I guess that's where you came in.'

'I thought Frank Benton said he'd changed his plans about your spread,' Harper said.

'He was lying, Brad, and I'm worried about Bob. Do you think they've tried to take him again?'

'I'll find out soon enough,' Harper replied. 'I was on my way to arrest Frank Benton when you showed up. I'll check the man who was following you. I rode him down. Stay close to me, Lily-Beth, and be ready to duck more flying lead, because I'm heading for a showdown. I've been sidetracked today, but that's over and I'm going for the men I want.'

Harper retraced his steps to where Lily-Beth's pursuer was lying motionless on the ground. He dropped to one knee to check him out. There was little he could see, and the only detail he ascertained was that the man was unconscious and breathing heavily. He remained motionless for some moments, thinking about what he had to do, then he arose.

'My horse sent him flying as I came up,' he said. 'It was too dark to see him, and he took a hard knock. You said two men took you from town, so what happened to the other one?'

'I don't know. It was getting dark. When my horse hit him he fell out of the saddle and his horse spooked and ran, so I guess he had trouble catching it again.' Lily-Beth reached out and grasped Harper's left elbow. 'You're not intending to brace Benton at his place on your own, are you? I think it would be smarter to go back to town for a posse. You couldn't possibly handle this trouble alone, Brad.'

Harper eased his aching body. He was exhausted, but his determination was as sharp as ever and he drew a deep breath.

'I know I should get help,' he allowed. 'But I've become accustomed to law dealing as and when required, and with no help.'

'But this business is highly organized, and you are greatly outnumbered,' Lily-Beth persisted. 'You'll get yourself killed if you go off half-cocked, and there won't be a lawman in the county to take out a posse.'

'I could certainly do with a dozen posse men right now.' Harper heaved a sigh and shook his head. 'I guess I ought to get smart for once and do like you say. I'm aware that I can't take you along with me to the Benton ranch because if I came off second best you'd be left at the mercy of those men. So we'd better make tracks back to town, Lily. Benton will still be around when I get back on the trail with a posse.'

The more he thought about it the better the change of plan appealed to him. He went to where Lily-Beth's horse was lying, realized that it was badly hurt, and put it out of its misery. He fetched the horse of the injured man and helped Lily-Beth into the saddle.

'What about that man?' Lily-Beth

demanded. 'Are you going to leave him here?'

'I can't take him along. He'll head for the Benton place if he comes back to his senses and I'll get him later. Let's get moving.'

They rode out. Harper set a fast pace across the darkened range towards the distant town. Frustration gripped him because he was unable to handle this investigation in his usual style, but he vowed to bring about a speedy conclusion to the crooked scheme.

The night relaxed its grip as dawn approached. Streaks of grey began to rake the sky and their range of vision increased. Harper was slumped in his saddle, his body stiff and sore. His left shoulder was protesting against the bullet burn he had received when he attacked Hoose, and he felt as if he had not slept for a week. As daylight began to filter across the range he roused himself and struggled mentally to become more alert. Looking around, he saw that they were within a mile or two of Clear Spring.

Lily-Beth became animated. She had remained silent during the long hours of the ride. Harper glanced at her, now he was able to see her face. She looked worn out, and he reaffirmed his intention to put an end to the crooked game which was being played in the county.

'Brad,' she said, 'I thought I heard hoofs behind us a while ago. I listened but didn't hear the sound again. Do you think we're being followed?'

'I'll soon find out.' Harper drew his pistol. 'Ride on ahead and keep going no matter what happens. I'll drop behind and check our back trail.'

'I'd rather stay with you,' Lily-Beth protested.

'And probably catch a stray slug,' he said. 'Push on, Lily. I'll catch up with you in a little while.'

He reined in and dismounted, trailed his reins and dropped to one knee. Lily-Beth rode on, and when she had passed out of earshot a heavy silence settled over the range. Harper stifled a yawn. His head was aching and he felt slightly feverish. He needed breakfast but there was no relief for him and he kept his attention upon the business in hand, holding his pistol ready.

Minutes passed and he heard nothing but the sighing of the wind in his ears. He canted his head and turned it slowly, listening intently. He was on the point of giving up and continuing when he caught the faint sound of a steel-shod hoof striking a stone somewhere close on his back trail. He thumbed back the hammer of his gun and drew a deep, steadying breath. Aware of the open range around him, he dropped flat on his belly in the long grass and waited, his frustration fleeing at the prospect of action.

Daylight was almost upon him. He could see now for a considerable distance, and he caught a movement in the haziness of the new day just seconds before a horse and rider materialized. The newcomer saw Harper's buckskin a moment or so later, reined in, then came forward more cautiously. He was carrying a rifle across his thighs; he lifted it into readiness.

Harper waited until the rider drew closer before getting to one knee. The man caught Harper's movement and his rifle began to lift. At the same moment a pistol fired at Harper from his right. He jerked round to see two men off to the side, apparently in cahoots with the man facing him. The silence of the early morning was shattered by raucous gunfire, and slugs smacked the ground about Harper.

The two men off to the right spurred their mounts directly at Harper, firing as they came. He kept low and concentrated on the rider directly behind. When he fired, the man seemed to leap in the air and he vacated his saddle with alacrity. He fired two quick shots at Harper as he landed on his feet, then ducked into cover. His bullets thudded into the ground beside Harper, who ignored the threat and turned his attention to the two approaching riders. They were coming in fast, both bent low over the necks of their mounts, their pistols flaming and blasting.

Harper was at a disadvantage but had no option but to stand and fight. He lifted his pistol, drew a bead on the left-hand rider, and fired. The man fell out of his saddle and bounced on the hard ground before lying motionless. Harper ducked lead from the surviving rider and rolled to another position to throw the man off aim, for the shots coming at him were too accurate for comfort. He felt pain flash through his left arm just above the elbow as a slug found him, but it did not inconvenience him; he pushed to his knees and prepared to sell his life dearly.

He took on the surviving rider coming from the right. In the split second before he fired he recognized the man in the early morning sunlight. It was Norton Calder, and Harper wondered where the man had been skulking since riding out of the Benton yard in full flight. He changed the angle of his muzzle as he recognized Calder, wanting the man alive if possible. His Colt .45 blasted. Calder dropped his gun immediately and swung away.

Harper shook his head, determined that Calder would not get away from him a second time. He aimed for Calder's horse and fired, hating the necessity of shooting an animal. The horse went down instantly in a slithering fall. Calder kicked his feet out of his stirrups and dived sideways out of his saddle to escape the fall. He fell awkwardly, started to get up, then dropped inertly.

A bullet jerked through the brim of Harper's Stetson. He turned to face the third man, who was on his feet and coming forward at a run, working the lever of his rifle and shooting fast from the hip. Harper snapped off a shot. The man faltered, paused, then lifted his rifle to his shoulder. Harper squeezed his trigger again, and the hammer struck an empty cartridge in his cylinder. He dropped flat instantly, desperately plucking a shell from a loop on his cartridge belt as the man came on once more.

But the man halted. Blood was staining the front of his shirt. His expression was hard, determined, but he was finding it difficult to fire again. His knees buckled and he sank slowly to the ground, remaining on his knees and attempting to work his rifle. Harper fumbled with his pistol as he hastily stuffed a fresh shell into the cylinder.

Harper closed his cylinder, lifted the pistol into the aim, and found he was looking into the muzzle of the opposing rifle. The man looked to be on his last legs, but he was determined to shoot Harper as he squinted through his sights. Harper fired as he threw himself flat. The rifle fired in the same instant, and the 44.40 slug went through the crown of Harper's Stetson, jerking it from his head. Harper's bullet struck the man in the centre of the chest, knocking him into a twisting fall.

It was over, Harper thought remotely. Three men had attacked him and all three were down. He attended to reloading his gun, and plucked a handful of fresh shells from the loops of his cartridge belt to thumb them into his cylinder, but hoofs were pounding the ground nearby. He looked up, expecting to see Lily-Beth returning, but he saw a small man in a brown store suit and wearing a flat-crowned Stetson approaching, holding a pistol in his right hand. The newcomer caught Harper flat-footed: gun open and fresh shells in his hand but none in the cylinder.

'Throw down your gun,' the man rapped. 'Deputy Sheriff Harper, I presume. They said you were hell on wheels and killing you was the only way to stop you.'

'Who in hell are you?' Harper demanded. 'I guess you're another in that sawmill set-up.'

'I'm Reuben Stross,' the man replied,

'boss of this business. Now get rid of your gun. I've got you dead to rights.'

Harper grimaced and tossed his gun on the ground, aware that there was no alternative. Stross had him cold.

10

'You've been playing hell with my set-up,' Stross accused, 'and no one was able to stop you. But I've got you now and you better say your prayers.'

Harper gazed at Stross, who was small and slightly built. Blue eyes stared back at him, and they were cold, unemotional, like the eyes of a rattle-snake. The hand holding the pistol seemed too small to work such a big weapon, but the muzzle did not waver in the slightest. Harper felt a pang of despair filter into his chest. He knew when he was beaten but tried to play for time because he had no other option.

'You don't expect to get away with this land steal, do you?' he demanded.

'I sure do.' Stross smiled. 'It has worked before, and it will succeed again in other parts when we have cleaned up around here. But you were like a burr under my saddle. I told Calder to take you out and he made a mess of it. But I won't make any mistake. With you dead there'll be no law left in this county. The sheriff was killed yesterday afternoon, and that crooked deputy, Kemp, is on our side. Now, with you gone, we'll have a clear run.'

As he spoke, Stross aimed his pistol at Harper's chest. Harper clenched his teeth. He was shocked by the news that the sheriff was dead. He had always been prepared to die in a shoot-out for the law, but to be shot down in cold blood was a horse of another colour. He tensed his muscles, determined to go down fighting, but Stross was well out of arm's reach and looked as if he knew one end of his gun from the other.

'There's nothing personal in this,' Stross said. 'I admire your nerve and skill, and I wish I had a dozen men like you.'

Harper closed his eyes. He felt like a rat caught in a trap. He heard a shot and flinched, but he was not touched by hot lead. He opened his eyes to see Stross falling forward across the neck of his horse, his gun spilling from his hand. Harper remained motionless until Stross hit the ground, then he snatched up his pistol. He heard hoofs approaching and swung round to see Lily-Beth riding towards him, her face set determinedly. She was waving a pistol and looked as if she were ready to take on the whole world.

'Are you OK, Brad?' she demanded. 'Did I do right? I had to shoot! I could see he was fixing to plug you.'

'You'll never do anything more right,' Harper replied. He bent over Stross, who was unconscious. Lily-Beth's bullet had been well aimed. Stross was bleeding in the chest, and it was spreading through the front of his white shirt. He opened Stross's shirt, and a sigh of relief escaped him. The wound was high in the chest and Stross should recover to stand trial. 'Lily, see what you can do for him — just stop the bleeding. I want to check on Calder. He's another I need to put before a judge.'

'Thank God we are not far from town,' Lily-Beth observed as she slid out of her saddle. 'We could do with some help.' She paused and considered for a moment. 'How many men do you think are left in this gang, Brad? You've been up to your knees in bodies since this started.'

'There'll be more around,' he responded wearily.

Lily-Beth dropped to her knees beside Stross. Harper turned to where Calder was lying motionless. He approached the man cautiously. Calder was unconscious with blood congealing around a superficial head wound just above his left ear. Harper searched him for weapons, found a two-shot pocket gun, and left him lying, aware that there was nothing he could for him. He went to check the other men who had attacked him. He found two dead and the third breathing his last.

Harper dropped to his knees beside

the dying man and spoke to him but could not call him back from the grim edge of death. Blood was bubbling sibilantly from the lung-shot that he had received. He was breathing laboriously, but not getting any air into his pierced lung. His eyes were closed but flickering. Blood was dribbling from a corner of his mouth. Even as Harper watched, the man expired with a shuddering sigh and relaxed to lie very stiff and still.

A strange weakness was slowly permeating Harper's body. He had to fight against the urge to lie down and close his eyes as if he, too, had been mortally wounded. He had to put his hands on the ground and lean his weight on them to remain steady. A buzzing sounded in his ears and his sight grew dim. Nausea crept stealthily through his stomach, and he mustered up what strength he could call upon in order to resist the encroaching sensation. He was aching in every muscle, and pain was attacking him through the wounds he had collected over the past two days.

'Brad, are you OK?' Lily-Beth called anxiously.

Harper made an effort to respond. He drew a deep breath and shook his head. His sight cleared and he looked around to see Lily-Beth coming towards him.

'I'm OK,' he replied. 'I'm just tired and hungry. We'll leave these men here and ride into town for help. Stross told me that Mort was killed yesterday afternoon.'

Lily-Beth uttered a cry of shock. Her face blanched. She turned away to climb into the saddle of a nearby horse and Harper mounted his buckskin. He looked around at the sprawled bodies as he shook his reins and set the horse into motion. They rode on silently, and fifteen minutes later they reached the outskirts of Clear Spring.

Harper slid out of his saddle in front of the law office. The street door stood ajar and Pete Halfnight appeared in the doorway at the sound of approaching hoofs. The town carpenter was holding a 12-gauge Greener double-barrelled shotgun. He gazed at Harper silently, his grim expression showing the state of his thoughts.

'Pete, is it true that Mort was shot dead yesterday?' Harper demanded.

'Yeah, and it happened right there on the sidewalk in front of the office. Two men were riding out of town with Lily-Beth.' Halfnight broke off when Lily-Beth appeared at Harper's shoulder. 'You got her back! Heck, Bob Fuller was shot in the livery barn as he saddled up to take out after her.'

Lily-Beth uttered a cry and clutched at Harper's arm.

'Is Bob OK?' she demanded.

'He's alive,' Halfnight responded, shaking his head, 'but the word is he'll be on his back for a month at least. He's at Doc's house.'

'I must go to him!' Lily-Beth turned instantly, but Harper grasped her arm.

'Hold on,' he rasped. 'You're not

going anywhere without me. Pete, get a posse together. There's a lot to be done. I want twenty men ready to ride in thirty minutes.'

'You look like you need the doctor, Brad,' Halfnight observed. 'What's been happening on the range?'

'I'll tell you later. Just get the men together and have them ready. I need to eat before I ride out.' He paused. 'Say, you've lived in town longer then I have, Pete — have you heard talk of a man named Buck Chilvers.'

Halfnight considered for a moment before shaking his head. 'I don't know the name,' he responded. 'Who is he?'

'If you don't know then we'll be wasting time talking about him. Send two posse men out on the north trail. They'll need to take a wagon. There was a shoot-out a short while ago, about two miles out of town, and a couple of men are down but still breathing. I want them brought in. They'll need Doc Carter's attention, and afterwards you can lock them in the cells. You'd better send two other men out to the Hoose trading post. Hoose is down with a busted leg, and Joss Kemp is also there, handcuffed. That'll be another wagon job. I want to see Hoose and Kemp in jail when I get back. I'll talk to the doc when I see him because he is gonna be a mite busy before we can get back to normal. Come on, Lily-Beth, let us go and see Bob.'

Lily-Beth clung to Harper's arm as they left the office. He paused on the sidewalk to look around. Someone had kicked dust over a bloodstain just outside the door, but not enough to disguise the grim reminder that Sheriff Bland had been gunned down in cold blood. Harper struggled to contain his emotions as they walked to the doctor's house. The town seemed quiet and normal, and he shook his head because he had been involved in a living nightmare for the past two days.

The bad dream continued at the doctor's house. Doc Carter insisted on treating Harper's injuries but Harper had his mind on what he had to do. He was feeling ill because he needed food, and after seeing Bob Fuller, who was unconscious in bed with a bullet through his chest, he left Lily-Beth in the doctor's care and departed to attend to his duties.

Possemen were already turning up at the law office, and Harper saw two of them head out of town with a wagon to pick up Stross and Calder. Satisfied that the big clean-up was under way. Harper went on to the diner to assuage his hunger, and afterwards saw another wagon heading out of town on its way to the trading post.

By the time he returned to the law office he was ready to continue. His duty was plain. He had to pick up Frank Benton. A crowd of possemen were standing around in front of the office, and Harper sent one of them to take his buckskin to the livery barn and fetch him a fresh horse.

'I want you to stay in town and keep

an eye on things, Pete,' Harper told Halfnight.

'I thought you might.' Halfnight shook his head. 'I'd rather ride with you and be where the action is.'

'You're the only man around I can trust to do as I say,' Harper replied. 'You'll have to stand in for the sheriff.'

'Nick Spenser looked in a few minutes ago,' Halfnight said. 'He'd heard that you were back in town. He told me to tell you that the town council want you to take over as sheriff and continue in the job until they can hold an election. And you're to pick yourself a deputy to take your place while you're acting as sheriff.'

'Do you want a deputy job?' Harper asked.

'I'll consider it.' Halfnight shrugged. 'I've been doing more posse work than carpentry lately.'

'You'll get more as a deputy than as a posse man,' Harper said. 'And while I'm out of town will you keep an eye on Lily-Beth for me? I'd like to think she'll be clear of trouble after this.'

'I'll take care of it,' Halfnight promised.

Harper went out to the street. The posse men were getting restless. The man sent to fetch Harper a fresh horse was leading one back along the street. Harper drew his pistol and checked it. He fetched a box of shells that Mort Bland had kept in his desk and refilled the empty loops on his cartridge belt. Relief filled him when he went back to the sidewalk and swung into the saddle of the fresh horse.

'We're riding to the Benton place to clean it out,' Harper said to the posse. 'With any luck we'll find the men I want skulking around there, but if they ain't then we'll search for them, and we won't come back to town until we've got them. Before we ride, does anyone know of a man called Buck Chilvers? It's possible he's living in the county under another name.'

The posse men looked at one another enquiringly, then shook their heads. Harper watched them intently. He sighed impatiently when no one came up with an answer.

'OK, let's raise dust,' he said, and touched spurs to his mount.

The posse moved out in a tight group. Townsfolk stood on the sidewalks to watch them leave town. Harper heaved a great sigh of relief as they cleared the community and he turned his thoughts to the job in hand. They passed the wagons heading out to collect the wounded and the dead, and Harper headed for the spot where he had left Stross and Calder. Motionless figures were stretched out in the sunlight where the fight had taken place. Calder was lying on his back. He was conscious when Harper dismounted and bent over him. Stross had moved closer to his henchman, and was lying on his side, unconscious.

'It looks like you've beaten us,' Calder observed.

'It is over for you!' Harper straightened. He turned to his waiting posse men.

'Joe,' he said. 'Have a couple of the posse stay with you and keep these two men company until the wagon arrives for them. Go back to town with them and guard them in the jail until I return.'

Two men prepared to follow Harper's orders, and Harper led the rest of the posse in the direction of the Benton spread. They rode at a mile-eating lope, and the sun was past its zenith when Harper saw the buildings of Frank Benton's ranch in the distance. He reined up out of sight of the spread and the posse dismounted to take a breather.

'I want six of you to circle to the rear of the house and catch anyone trying to make a run for it when I ride into the yard,' Harper said. 'Give them a chance to surrender but don't let anyone get away. Hank, pick five men and get moving. I'll wait here ten minutes before moving. That should give you time to get into position.'

Six of the posse men departed.

Harper watched them riding in a wide circle around the ranch until they were out of sight. He lounged on the grass and closed his eyes. Tiredness tugged at him, and his mind felt drugged by the lack of sleep, but he was gripped by a grim determination to finish this business. He forced his mind to consider his next move.

The remaining posse men were checking their guns. There was not much conversation as they awaited the order to ride into action. Harper climbed into his saddle when he reckoned the cut-off party had settled into position, and he motioned for the posse men to follow him.

Their hoofs drummed on the hard range. Harper eased his pistol in its holster and straightened his shoulders. They rode into the ranch yard. Harper saw a man carrying a rifle appear in the open doorway of the barn, gaze at their approach for some moments, and then make a run for the ranch house. Harper drew his pistol and cocked it as he ordered the posse to spread out. They rode across the yard to the porch of the house, and at that moment gunfire sounded from the back yard.

Harper dismounted and lunged across the porch. The front door was ajar; he hit it with his shoulder and entered quickly, his gun levelled. The posse men followed him closely. Shots were hammering out back and Harper made for the kitchen. A bullet smacked into woodwork close to his left shoulder and he saw a figure lurking in the kitchen doorway. Gunsmoke was swirling. Another shot was fired in Harper's direction and he triggered his pistol in swift reply. The figure dropped out of sight. Harper halted.

'This is the law,' he called stridently. 'Throw down your guns, raise your hands, and come out into the open.'

A hand holding a pistol appeared around the kitchen door and fired repeatedly until the hammer struck an empty cartridge. Harper and the posse men ducked and prepared to fight.

Harper fired three spaced shots into the kitchen door. The house shook to the quick gun blasts and gunsmoke drifted. Harper saw a man stagger from behind the door and drop limply to the floor. As he went forward the shooting ceased and an uneasy silence settled over the house. Excited voices were shouting out back, and Harper kicked open the inner kitchen door to find the kitchen deserted except for the two men he had shot.

Harper moved to the kitchen window. He could see three of his posse men outside, standing with guns upraised. He attracted their attention, then went out to the yard. He found three bodies lying on the ground with Al Garrod bending over one of them. Garrod was highly elated.

'They are dead — didn't want to give in,' Garrod said. 'We gave them a chance when they came out of the kitchen but they started shooting so we cut them down. Have you got the man you are looking for, Brad?'

'He's not here,' Harper replied. 'I guessed it would be too easy to walk in and catch him flat-footed. But I don't think he's left the county. These badmen are certain they are going to succeed in their plan to steal range. We'll search the place, and then I'll look for tracks to follow.'

'Do you know what the guy looks like?' Garrod persisted.

'I know him by sight. Get the men organized, Al. Check around and see if there's anyone else here. I'll look for tracks over by the corral. And tell the men to keep out of sight. If anyone spots us as they come in they'll high-tail it for sure. Put our horses in the barn and leave a man to watch them.'

Harper walked around the house and headed for the corral. He studied the ground for tracks, and saw recent prints of three horses heading away from the ranch. He studied the tracks until he was certain he would know them again before following them a short distance to assess the general direction in which

252

they were heading. He was standing on the open trail outside the ranch yard when he heard hoofs approaching. It was too late for him to hunt cover, and he stood with his right hand down at his side, watching a rider coming towards the ranch.

The man was a stranger, Harper noted, and when the newcomer drew nearer he regarded Harper with suspicion.

'Who in hell are you?' he demanded as he halted before Harper, his hand on the butt of his pistol.

'I'm the deputy out of Clear Spring,' Harper replied. He gave no sign of hostility but his right hand was ready to make a fast draw.

The man relaxed. 'I heard we had a pet deputy on the pay roll,' he declared.

'Every gang of outlaws should have one,' Harper responded.

'Is Benton around?'

'No. He rode out early this morning. Get down and come on in to wait for him.'

The man shook his head. 'I can't stay. I've got to get on to town to talk to the men running the sawmill. Maybe you'll give Benton a message when you see him.'

'Sure. I've got to stick around until he shows up.'

'Tell him Buck Chilvers is taking over the set-up and everyone is to pull out. The game is busted flat around here. Head for Abilene and Chilvers will see everyone there. It'll mean a fresh start somewhere else.'

Harper tensed at the mention of Buck Chilvers. 'Who in hell is Buck Chilvers?' he demanded.

'You must have heard of him?' the man said.

'Sure I have, but he's living around here under a different name, and I'd like to know who he really is.'

'It ain't for me to say. He's spent years living down his past. Now I've got to be riding. There'll be hell to pay if Benton doesn't get out fast.'

Harper waited until the man began

to turn his horse and then drew his pistol. The rider looked down when he heard the weapon being cocked and froze in shock.

'You ain't going anywhere,' Harper grated. 'Get off that horse and keep your hand away from your gun.'

'What the hell! Ain't you Joss Kemp?'

'No I'm the other deputy — Brad Harper — the honest one. Now get down or I'll shoot you out of the saddle.'

The man dismounted and Harper disarmed him.

'Where have you come from?' Harper demanded.

'Do you expect me to tell you?' the man countered.

'I won't worry about it. Get moving. You'll wait for Benton to show up whether you like it or not.'

'You won't get away with this. I'm scouting for a dozen riders waiting behind that rise over there and if they don't get my signal that the ranch is deserted they'll come riding in here hell for leather, and they are loaded for bear.'

'That's the best news I've heard all day.' Harper nodded. 'Give them the signal. Tell them to come on in. I'll be glad to see them. But don't give the wrong signal because you'll be the first to take a slug if trouble starts.'

'You're not alone here!' Realization showed on the man's weathered features as he glanced searchingly at the ranch buildings, but all of the posse men were under cover.

'Get moving,' Harper said, 'across the yard and into the house.'

'You'll be cut down before you get twenty yards,' the man warned.

Harper nudged him with the muzzle of his pistol. 'You won't make another step if you don't move now,' he threatened.

They started across the yard to the house. They had barely made four strides when a bullet kicked up dust beside Harper's left foot and the sound of a rifle shot shattered the heavy silence. Harper reacted instantly. He grasped his prisoner, stepped behind him, and continued towards the house, using him as a shield. A fusillade of shots racked the silence and dust sprang up around them. They reached the porch and Harper saw some of his posse men standing at the windows inside the house with guns ready.

The door of the house was opened and Al Garrod peered out. He was holding a rifle.

'Come on in, Brad,' he called. 'We're ready for them. Half the posse is in the barn. They'll open fire when we do.'

Bullets began thudding into the front of the house. Harper dragged his prisoner along as he dashed for the open door, and Garrod slammed the door when they were inside.

'Someone put handcuffs on this guy and watch him,' Harper ordered. He turned to the nearest window and peered out. His eyes gleamed when he saw a group of ten riders appearing on the trail outside the yard. 'Hold your fire and we'll see what they've got in mind.'

The riders cantered into the yard. Sunlight glinted on their drawn guns. Harper recognized Frank Benton in the lead, and wondered where the crooked rancher had found this crew. He looked more intently at the riders, and was surprised when he recognized some of them as Abe Hickman's outfit from the AH spread. Then he spotted a rider in the background, hanging back in the brush, but before he could get a good look at the man the riders in the yard began shooting at the house, certain that he was alone and attempting to overwhelm him.

'OK,' he yelled. 'Open fire!'

Pistols and rifles cut loose and a hail of lead swept the yard. Men tumbled out of their saddles and horses bucked and ran. The posse men in the barn joined in shooting, and Harper watched grimly as the riders were cut down. At least half their number fell from their saddles and the remainder raised their hands in surrender. Harper noted that Frank Benton was one of the survivors as he headed for the back door of the house.

'Take the survivors prisoner, Al,' he instructed Garrod. 'There's a man out there I'm anxious to talk to.'

He left the house and ran across to the barn. The big door was open and posse men stood within its cover, all holding rifles and covering the yard.

'Two of you hit your saddles and come with me,' Harper ordered. 'There is a man beyond the ridge outside the yard whom I need to catch.'

They mounted up and rode out across the yard. Harper set a fast pace, watching the top of the rise as he ascended. The man who had watched the fight in the yard from here had now departed. Harper kept riding, flattened over the neck of his horse until he hit the crest, where he pulled his mount to a swerving halt. His keen gaze alighted on a rider who was galloping away.

Harper jerked his Winchester from its

scabbard, jacked a cartridge into the breech, and aimed at the fleeing man. He fired a single shot and the horse went down. The rider kicked his feet clear of his stirrups, hit the ground hard and remained inert. Harper galloped forward, covering the motionless figure. The man began to stir as Harper reached him. Harper stepped down from his saddle, thrust the Winchester into its boot, and drew his pistol.

The man sat up and held a hand to his head. It was Abe Hickman, and he gazed at Harper in shocked silence.

'Buck Chilvers?' Harper challenged.

Hickman did not reply. He shook his head and shrugged.

'You staged the jailbreak in town,' Harper continued. 'So who killed Redfern afterwards and put him in Sim Archer's store?'

'He wanted out, and that was the only way.' Hickman shook his head. 'I never wanted back into the business but I was forced, so Redfern had no choice, and that's why he died.'

Harper covered the rancher, ordered him to his feet, and rode hard on him back to the ranch. It came to him then that the echoes fading into the distance were from his last shot in this grim business. Questions had yet to be answered, but he was now in a position to ask them. The posse men had taken four prisoners, who were being handcuffed, and Harper felt tension running out of him as he looked around. It was over now, and there was nothing left to do but rake through the ashes for the truth of the business and ensure that justice was done.

THE END

We do hope that you have enjoyed reading this large print book.

Did you know that all of our titles are available for purchase?

We publish a wide range of high quality large print books including:
Romances, Mysteries, Classics
General Fiction
Non Fiction and Westerns

Special interest titles available in large print are:
The Little Oxford Dictionary
Music Book, Song Book
Hymn Book, Service Book

Also available from us courtesy of Oxford University Press:
Young Readers' Dictionary
(large print edition)
Young Readers' Thesaurus
(large print edition)

For further information or a free brochure, please contact us at:
Ulverscroft Large Print Books Ltd.,
The Green, Bradgate Road, Anstey,
Leicester, LE7 7FU, England.
Tel: (00 44) **0116 236 4325**
Fax: (00 44) **0116 234 0205**

VENGEANCE RIDES THE RIVER

Hugh Martin

The murder of Dave Lockhart's wife, by desperados who plague the Red River country of Texas, results in his desperate mission for revenge. Lockhart is no natural killer, but his quest for revenge becomes marked by murder, bullets and gun-smoke, and brings him face to face with deadly men. Then he meets Helen, who must overcome difficulties that few women ever face. Now she must teach Lockhart that there can be a world of difference between vengeance and justice . . .

DOC DRYDEN, GUNSLINGER

Ted Rushgrove

Clay Dryden, one of the band of outlaws known as the Sankey gang, is challenged to a gunfight by the brother of the gang leader and kills him. Finding that there were no bullets in his brother's revolver, Sankey vows to avenge his death. Then, in the town of Crossville, Sankey finds the former outlaw has set up a medical practice. Will Dryden be spared? It seems that Clay's future as the town's doctor hangs in the balance . . .

WADE'S WAR

Chet Cunningham

It's 1865 and the Civil War is ending. On their small Missouri farm outlaws murder Wade Tretter's parents. Fourteen-year old Wade sells the few cattle remaining and heads west to find the killers. After killing two of them in an act of retribution, Wade finds the last two men posing as model citizens in a small Kansas town. How can he beat the odds and bring these powerful men to justice without hurting their new families?

SILENT WOMAN SHOWDOWN

M. C. Young

Tom Bantry can't understand why the pretty Cora Lee won't give him the time of day, especially after he rescued her from a man like Rufus Earle. But Tom has other problems to think about. He stands to lose his ranch to the Earle brothers while his friend Silas Sidwell hopes to benefit from the chaos the trouble-makers cause. Ultimately, Cora Lee will have a crucial role to play in bringing things to a head when the time comes . . .